Teenage Castaways

By Jessica Cohn

Part 1: Arrival

CHAPTER 1: 4 DAYS BEFORE SHIPWRECK

Four boys, four girls, one two week cruise. It may seem like every seventeen year old girl's dream, but it was my worst nightmare. I never cared for boats. In fact you could say I hated them. You would only catch me on one if it was for a forty five minute whale watch, never for a two week cruise. The only reason I was even going on the stupid cruise was because my dad had decided he had enough of me that summer. He figured two weeks away from him would make him be able to stand me more. Ever teen going on the trip won it from their school's contest. My school, Wisconsin Heights High School, didn't do a contest. But, a different school in Cambridge Massachusetts backed out at the last minute. My dad forced me into pretending that I was from Cambridge High so I could go on the trip. Or more importantly so I could be away from him.

Ever since my mother died two years ago, and even before, my dad played poker every night and went to bars. It wasn't too pleasant to hear him come home drunk every night. Now, sometimes another person in tow. So, I guess I was kind of glad to be out of the house. Just not on a two week cruise around the Caribbean.

Stepping on to the platform of the boat, I turned and waved to my dad. He was sober for once and with his graying hair, he looked almost innocent. But I knew better. My dad gave a half hearted wave and turned to leave. Sighing, I grabbed my duffle bag of clothes and headed to cabin 2B.

Flinging open the door to the claustrophobic cabin, I glanced cautiously inside. Four bunk beds were lined up against two bleach white walls while a chest of drawers and a grainy porthole were on the other wall of the cabin. Looking beside the door that I had just come through, a door to a tiny bathroom was open. Cool, our own private bathroom. A tingle went up my spine as I thought about the girls that would share the cabin with me. I meandered over to the nearest bottom bunk bed. I had a tendency to roll out of bed so I was *not* sleeping on the top bunk.

"What do you think you're doing?" A girl's sharp voice rang out in the small cabin. I jumped in surprise. I twisted away from the bed and looked at the open cabin door. The girl was physically beautiful. She had long golden blonde hair and her body was completely built for a super model. Her icy blue eyes were pierced on mine, making it hard to look away.

"I have to have the bottom bunk," The girl said, gesturing to the bunk where my bag was.

"There are two bottom bunks," I pointed to the one that was across from mine. She huffed and gave me an evil glare.

"I don't like that one," The girl claimed, still glaring at me. Hesitantly I picked up my bag and moved it to the other bunk bed. I was in no mood to fight with the girl.

"So what's your name anyway?" She asked as she began to unpack her bag. Oh wait, I mean *bags*.

"Monica," I said and extended my hand towards her. She grimaced.

"I'm Bethany but don't even think about calling me Beth," She said and looked at my hand as if it had rabies.

4

"I wouldn't dare," I said sarcastically and pulled my hand away. While her back was turned, I rolled my emerald green eyes. The ship wasn't that big. It held the four girls, the four boys, the crew and the trip leader. If I had to be stuck on the boat for two weeks with her, there was no way I was going to be around her when we went to the islands. I was so going to need a break from her. I already did and I've known her for exactly three and a half minutes! I was going to scream.

The clatter of a suitcase rolling down the hallway drifted in and I turned to see the next arrival of our group. The first thing I saw was the long skirt before I saw the rest of the girl.

"Hello," The girl said in a heavy British accent. The girl had black hair as straight as stick and wore a school uniform, which, judging by the skirt was Catholic. Plus, she wore a mall silver chain around her neck that held a tiny cross.

"My name is Emilia," She said and put her suitcase on the bunk above Bethany's. "I'm from Catholic Heart High School. I grew up in England but transferred to Maine last year. That's why I qualified for this trip. Where are you from?"

"Sea Bay High in Florida," Bethany said with a flip of her hair. Well, that sure explained her looks.

"Cambridge High in Massachusetts," I answer nonchalantly while looking into Emilia's green eyes. I hate lying almost as much as I hate boats.

"Brilliant!" She exclaimed and clapped her hands. "And what are your names?"

"Bethany," She says with another flick of her hair. That was seriously getting annoying.

5

"I'm Monica," I waved. The boat's horn blew and I knew from the movies that it meant we were leaving.

"Oh I can tell were all going to be such good friends," Emilia giggled and started picking things out of her suitcase. Tough panting came from the hallway.

"I'm here! I'm here!" A girl with deep chestnut brown curly hair and light brown skin entered the cabin and bent over, panting. She wore light weight sweats and was obviously an athlete. A thin layer of sweat covered her bronze forehead. She must have run a long way if she was out of breath.

"I'm Caroline," the girl said and stood up straight. She swiped her hand across her forehead, disposing of the sweat. "I'm from California."

"I'm Monica," I greeted and pointed out the other girls in the room. Caroline came in and closed the door behind her.

At dinner, we met the boys. At the circular table across from us, they were already laughing and throwing food at each other like they were already best friends. Typical. They had sports and stuff to bond over. We had fashion magazines and makeup to bond over. I wasn't interested in either.

"Hello girls! I'm the director of this program, Diane. It's so nice to meet you!" A heavy set woman with blonde hair came over to our table with a clipboard in her chubby hands. She was dressed in the uniform for all crew: khaki shorts with a blue polo. "We're all going to introduce ourselves in a minute so here's what you need to say." She handed us each a laminated index card that read:

PLEASE STATE YOUR:

FIRST AND LAST NAME:

AGE:

SCHOOL:

FAVORITE THING TO DO:

Was she serious? This was like we were in the third grade again! I groaned. Diane seemed like the kind of person who would make me do this even if I protested.

"Alright boys and girls, listen up!" Diane tried to get our attention from the middle of the cafeteria. I turned my gaze towards her.

"Welcome to the two week cruise through the Caribbean for straight A students! Before dinner is served, we are going to play a little get to know you game. Let's start with the boys," Diane explained and gestured for the m to start. A guy with blonde brown hair that fell gently over one eye headed to the center of the dining room.

"I guess I'll go first," he said in a soft but strong voice. It was a voice that could make any girl go weak in the knees, like me. I glanced around our round table. From the looks on the girls' faces, it looks like they melted like I did.

"I'm Colby Marshalls and I'm seventeen years old. I go to West Brooke High School in Colorado and my favorite thing to do is play football," Colby informed us and sat back down at his table. Us girls sighed dreamily. The boy that was sitting next to, sigh, Colby stood up. He looked slightly dorky and was averagely tall.

His black hair came right to the middle of his forehead and his eyes were a brilliant shade of blue.

"Uh, hi. My name is Nick Brady. I'm seventeen and I go to Williamsburg Academy in Virginia. My favorite thing to do is play soccer," Nick said and blushed. Him? Playing soccer? I was so busy laughing to myself that I didn't realize the next boy had gone up until he cleared his throat. I glanced at Nick. His head was dipped, listening to the boy. He must have felt my gaze on him because he lifted his head and locked eyes with me. The boy could be a dork, but he had the most amazing eyes I had ever seen. Nick, his name was, smiled a shy smile and dipped his head back down. He didn't even give me the chance to smile back.

"My favorite thing to do is work on my family's farm," the boy that was in the center of the room finished in a sweet southern accent. I completely missed the first part of his speech. He had red hair with lots of freckles and was definitely strong. You could see his muscles bulge when he moved his arms.

"What was his name?" I whispered to Caroline as the last boy stood up.

"Calvin," Caroline whispered back and turned her attention back to the center of the cafeteria.

"My name is Bidzill Browne which means "he is strong" in Native American. I'm seventeen and I go to school on my home reservation in New Mexico. My favorite thing to do is shoot bows and arrows," Bidziil sat back down. His name didn't match him. He looked thin, not strong at all. I would have been surprised if he could lift weights. Maybe Calvin and Bidziil should switch names.

"Thank you boys. Girls, you heard the guys, now it's your turn," Diane said turning to our table. "Who would like to go first?" I gulped. A quick glance around the table told me that everyone was nervous except Bethany. She was looking at herself in a compact mirror. Vain.

"Bethany why don't you go first?" Diane suggested. Bethany looked up happily.

"Sure! Why not?" Bethany flounced to the middle of the room and gave a little wave to Colby.

"My name is Bethany Stewart. Not Beth. I'm sixteen and I go to Sea Bay High in Florida. My favorite thing to do is shop!" Bethany smiled and gave another wave like we were in a theme park and she was the main attraction. I rolled my eyes again. I glanced over at Emilia and Caroline. Emilia looked a little green and Caroline had shrunk in her seat. It seemed like I was next. The second Bethany sat down, I stood and made my way to the center of the room. It wasn't that easy considering the boat was moving. I took a deep breath, held my card and began.

"My name is Monica Jacobs. I'm seventeen years old and I go to Cambridge High in Massachusetts. My favorite thing to do is listen to my Ipod," I finished my speech and headed back to the table. That wasn't so bad. Emilia still looked a little green though. I whispered across the table,

"Emilia don't be nervous. It was hardly worth getting worked up over." She looked at me and slowly shook her head.

"I'm not green because of saying a speech, I'm green because I'm seasick," She said and I paled. Sitting down you could really feel the motion of the water. To get my mind off the waves,

I fixed my attention on Caroline who was now at the center of the room.

"My name is Caroline Reed. I'm seventeen years old and I go to North Gate High in California. My favorite thing to do is also play soccer," She said while twirling her hair. Emilia was next. She got up shakily and stumbled to the front of the room.

"My name is Emilia and…" was all she said before she let out a green spew of vomit.

That night was absolutely horrible. After the incident, Emilia was sent back to the cabin and we were served a dinner of fried chicken, fries and mashed potatoes. Bethany refused to eat it. When dinner was over we headed back to our cabins to sleep. The boys' cabin was adjacent to ours so we had to be extra careful about making sure the door was shut and locked before we changed for bed. With the waves rocking the boat, it was extremely hard to brush my teeth and spit in the tiny bathroom. Emilia held a pot next to her which she kept puking in. Bethany didn't look happy at all considering she had her bunk right underneath Emilia's. Then again, she wasn't looking that well herself. She had applied a green face mask that she said "cleansed her pores" and put in hair curlers. If that wasn't enough, she also wore an eye mask. It was June not Halloween. I wasn't feeling too well either. My bed was hard and lumpy with odd little springs poking into my back. Worse, Caroline kept tossing and turning which caused her bed springs to squeak way too often. I laid awake just listening to everyone's breathing. It wasn't long until I couldn't even hear Emilia's puking. I got up slowly, careful not to shake the bed. Throwing my blue robe on over my purple tank top and grey shorts I eased open the door to our cabin and stepped barefoot into the hall. Climbing the stairs to the deck was easier than earlier. Before, the steps wobbled with my new sea legs. This time, they stayed still.

I didn't expect to see anyone else on the deck knowing it was past the eleven o'clock curfew. But, standing at the railing dressed boxer shorts and a white t-shirt was Colby. At first, I thought it was Captain Bernard but then I realized the Captain probably wouldn't be wearing boxer shorts. I had passed the boys' cabin and heard a chorus of snores coming from it. I figured they had all been asleep. Apparently they weren't. Colby shifted his weight and I couldn't help staring at the leanness of his body.

"Hey Colby right?" I carefully asked, making sure I wasn't drooling.

"Yeah. I didn't expect to see anybody else up here," he said, gesturing to the deck.

"Me neither. I'm Monica," I said, extending my hand. He smiled and his teeth gleamed a blinding white.

"I know. You said your name at dinner," Colby laughed as he shook my hand and I blushed a deep velvety red.

"Oh. I didn't think you would remember. So what are you doing out here? It's past curfew you know," I asked and turned to the salt covered railing.

"I could ask you the same thing. I love the sound of the waves. It just seems so peaceful out here. When I was little, my family took me to the shore every summer as our one vacation since we didn't live near a beach. I guess the waves are like a connection to home somehow," Colby said and I was very aware of the quick shooting glances he was giving me out of the corner of his eye. "Did you really think I wouldn't remember your name?" I blushed again.

"Yeah. You just seem like the kind of guy who likes beauty over substance," Colby looked at me with a twisted face.

"Well I don't," Colby said quietly and pushed off the railing, heading towards the cabins. I guess I offended him and I definitely did not want to do that.

"Colby wait. I'm sorry. My mother died when I was fifteen so I'm not very trusting of other people. My friends Kayce and Rachel tell me I judge people too quickly," I told to Colby's back. I felt vulnerable to Colby. Just his very presence made me want to pour my heart out to him. That feeling was strange to me. Colby turned to look at me.

"I'm sorry," he said quietly again and walked away. I stood there at the railing, feeling the ocean spray, for a long time before I headed back to my cabin. Colby and I seemed to connect somehow but I still wasn't comfortable with that vulnerable feeling. But I liked Colby. And maybe, just maybe, he liked me back.

So far the cruise was actually fun. Throughout the day we had special activities that surrounded our interests such as dolphin watching, playing poker, watching movies or in Bethany's case sunbathing. I wasn't afraid then. When I was in my cabin at night with all the girls sleeping soundly, I was afraid. Sometimes I found myself wandering the deck at night, feeling the salty sea spray. It was a place that I could confront my fears and be alone where no one would see me cry.

I never cry at funerals. There, you're in a state of shock, constant questions running through your head. Like the questions that ran through mine and still do. Why did my mother leave me here on Earth? Did my father *have* to start drinking? And the worst, would my life be any different if my mother was here today? Something told me no. As I stood on the deck, my fingers clutching the railing, horrific images passed through my brain. My father when he would come home drunk, my mother yelling at him, asking how he could be so irresponsible. How my father would get careless and bruises would show up on her face the next day. She told everyone she ran into something or fell out of bed and tried to cover them up with makeup, but I knew the truth. Then came the fateful night where I lived and she didn't.

I was sitting in bed doing science homework when I was fifteen. My mother came in with tears streaming down her beautiful face and two duffle bags in her hands.

"Come on honey, pack up as much clothing as you can. We're going to Grandma's," She said and threw me a bag. I knew better than to ask what was going on. My dad was home but he was nowhere in sight. That couldn't last long. My mom raced us out to the car and I hopped in the back because there were some carelessly thrown magazines on the passenger seat and we didn't have time to move them. Panic was coursing through my veins as I buckled my seat belt. My dad came bursting out of the house screaming. He was drunk. Again. I tightened my seat belt as we pulled out of the driveway. My mother, terrified he would catch us, didn't buckle hers. Our car raced down the street coming up to the nearest intersection that would take us to my Grandma's. She had no idea what went on in our house or that we were coming over. I was thinking about the unfinished homework left on my bed when my mom slammed the brakes on. Our car crashed head first into another car. My seat belt saved me. My mother's unbuckled one did not. I remember being pulled out of the damaged car and being loaded into an ambulance. I looked around for my mom, but I didn't see her. They had already taken the body away. I got away with a broken arm. The other driver needed stitches and had a broken leg. My mother was gone.

I awoke on the morning of our third day at sea to gulls cackling. I stood up and stretched my back. As I went into the bathroom to brush my teeth, I noticed something odd. There wasn't constant movement under my feet and I heard only the sound of waves lapping against the shore. *Shore*. Rushing over to the window, I saw the island with its tall peak of the mountain, the hustle on shore where people were lounging on chairs and sipping fruity drinks, and the beauty of the tropical flowers. It was truly magical.

"Wake up! We're at the first island!" I shouted and shook Caroline. Her brown eyes snapped open and she sat straight up, startled by my voice.

"The first island? Yes!" She yelled and catapulted out of bed. Together we woke up Bethany and Emilia and the four of us hurried to get dressed in beach gear. I threw my brown hair up into a messy ponytail. Like every other day, we were required to meet Diane on the deck to go over the day's agenda at eight o'clock sharp. It was seven fifty seven.

"Hurry!" Emilia wailed while tripping over her skirt.

"Emilia, are you seriously going to wear that to the beach?" I asked. The girl was going to get heatstroke!

"Well yes, I'm in my bathing suit," She looked at me confused. I just shrugged and followed the girls down the hall. When reached the deck, the boys were already whooping and hollering to get on shore.

"Now now boys, settle down. Ah look! The girls are here. Ok now, everybody listen up," Diane instructed while holding her clipboard out in front of her. "Okay, so as you can see, today we will be going on to island number one that has a name I can't pronounce," we giggled, "so. You all have three hours in the morning to hang out on the beach which will start as soon as we get to shore. Then we will have lunch at Hotel Paradise at eleven o'clock. After that, we are going on a hike through the forest where you will learn about many native animals and plants that live on the Caribbean islands. Then you have time to do whatever you want. But, tonight you must meet on the beach for the native campfire. Then we will retire to our cabins and set sail the next morning. Got it?" She rattled off. We nodded, eager to get on to

15

land. "Okay pile in," Diane said indicating the small speed boat that was stationed below. The guys jumped on board, jostling the boat and rocking the waves.

"Careful! This boat was a gift!" The man who was driving the colorful speed boat gruffly scolded in a thick accent I couldn't place. Us girls got in more delicately. I sung my leg over the side of the boat and then the other. When I was dangling by my arms, I let go, hoping that I would land on the boat. I did with a mild thump. But unfortunately, Diane wasn't as lucky as I was. She plummeted into the sliver of water between the two boats.

"Well!" Diane scoffed as she dragged her wet body on to the boat. We all laughed, Bidzill in particular, who had a funny laugh. The driver sped the boat away, heading towards paradise. Literally. I may not have wanted to come on the stupid trip, but I definitely wanted to hike and lay on the beach.

My toes dug into the sand. A tiny sand crab crawled across my big toe. I silently begged it not to bite me. The bits of sand grain tickled my fingers and I reached down to grab a handful. What was that old saying; when life gives you lemons, make lemonade? What was my lemonade? I've had plenty of lemons in my life, but they must all be too sour to make lemonade. What good could come out of this trip? I would much rather be babysitting a bratty kid down the street then be here. Well okay, here on the trip not the beach. The only person that I had talked to and actually liked was Caroline. But what did we have in common? She was all sporty and athletic and well, cool. I just wasn't.

The sun was blazing on my body when a shadow fell over me.

"Hey, you're blocking my sun," I mumbled. My one piece diving team bathing suit shifted as I attempted to move back into the sun.

"Don't start sounding like Bethany or I will go nuts. You're the only other sane girl here," Caroline's voice broke me out of my trance.

"Oh hey, I didn't know it was you. What's up?" I asked pulling myself into a sitting position on my beach towel.

"It's time for the hike. I'm surprised you finished lunch so fast just to come out here again before the hike," Caroline stepped to the side, bringing back my sun.

"I just wanted a little time to be alone without the guys being constantly around," I said while standing up and pulling my t-shirt over my bathing suit and shorts. When we had our three hours of beach time, the guys headed off along the edge of the beach to play Frisbee which they "accidentally" threw in our direction multiple times. Bethany kept talking obnoxiously, Emilia was humming and Caroline was practicing soccer. It was all too much. I just needed some time without anyone around to enjoy some peace. So after our lunch of salmon and fruit, I rushed back out to the beach.

"Okay, but now were going on the hike and I know that you don't want to miss that," Caroline tempted and I anxiously followed her to where our group was.

I thought the hike would be fun. I thought that we would learn about the native plants and animals while spending time in the fresh mountain air. Boy was I wrong. The guide just droned on and on about the most boring things. I did not need to know how to identify possum poop! I thought the only two people who actually cared about what the guide was saying was Bidziil and Nick. No surprise there. Even Diane looked utterly bored. The only interesting part was when the guide told us about their most feared predator, the jaguar. He told us ways the jaguar would sneak up on creatures and if it was hungry, it would eat anything that moved. He also said that there were fences that kept the jaguars out so we had no need to worry. Not like I was anyway.

By the time the campfire had come around, I was already exhausted. Caroline and I spent the remainder of the day walking along the beach in search of cool shells or tidal pools. We found none. But we did try one of the fruity drinks the locals were serving. Mine was papaya.

"That's our group there," Caroline pointed to the huge glow of a fire in the distance.

"Okay great. At least we won't have to walk anymore," I complained. My feet were killing me. We made it to our group and I sat down between Colby and Caroline on the sand. Our group was gathered around the campfire with tourists and locals. The locals that were hosting were dressed in feathers and crazy masks.

"I heard this is supposed to be awesome," Colby whispered to me. His breath smelled fruity and I suspected he had one of the drinks as well.

"I hope so. I'm in the mood for something fun," I whispered back. Drums began to play and the show began. The locals preformed a dance that they said brought light to the dark night and scared away the predators. Then we all talked while they roasted a pig. When we were finished, they had us join in the dance and we had to put on crazy headdresses with more feathers. I thought we'd never get back to our cabins.

The campfire finally ended around midnight. All eight of us were incredibly tired as we trudged our way into our cabins. Caroline, Bethany, Emilia and I collapsed onto our bunks. I sighed.

"As much as I'd like to lay here, I want to get to sleep as quickly as possible," Caroline said and pulled her pajamas out of her suitcase. Just as she was about to take her shirt off,

"Your door's open!" Nick called out from their cabin. Like I said before, if both cabins had our doors open, we could see into each other's. Caroline screamed loudly and hurriedly shut the door. The boy's laughter could still be heard through it. Caroline braced her back against the door and breathed a sigh of relief. She continued getting into her pajamas. Without getting into mine, I crawled underneath the covers. The anchored ship rocking in the waves lulled me into a dreamless sleep.

The next evening, our group was sitting in the cafeteria, playing meaningless games while it poured outside and thunder cracked. Every time it rumbled we all jumped. We were all scattered throughout the room in groups. Caroline, Calvin and I were playing the board game Monopoly, Nick, Emilia and Bidziil were playing Scrabble and Colby and Bethany were Poker. I suspected it would have been Strip Poker if Diane wasn't hovering.

"Monica it's your turn," Calvin passed me the dice. A rolled a three and moved my object to the correct space. Thunder rumbled outside again and a wave crashed into the side of the boat. Suddenly, a loud speaker from somewhere in the dining room came on.

"Attention passengers, please go to your cabins and stay there until further notice. Staff, we need you up front immediately. Thank you," The speaker shut off. I glanced around confused at the rest of us. They looked as confused as I felt. We all looked at Diane.

"Hmm," She said, puzzled like the rest of us, "I guess we should follow the instructions." Diane left us and headed to the front deck with the rest of the staff. The rest of us headed to our cabins.

Bethany, Emilia, Caroline and I sat on our bunk beds in silence. Bethany was reading a fashion magazine, Caroline had her soccer ball that she was bouncing, Emilia was reading her bible and I stared at the bottom of the bunk above me. It had been a good twenty minutes and nothing had happened yet. Rain was pelting the outside and I pitied the captain. Who would want to steer the boat in that weather? The thunder was as loud as ever and I almost didn't hear the knock on our cabin door. It was soft and muted. I opened the wood door to find all four boys outside, their shoes wet.

"Can we come in? Our cabin is flooding," Nick asked, acting slightly frantic.

"How is your cabin flooding and ours isn't?" I asked, "We're on the same level." The boys hustled in and we were overcrowded in the tiny cabin.

20

"Do you notice anything about the furniture?" Nick asked us. I glanced around the room and found that everything was leaning slightly to the right.

"Oh my god, everything's tilted!" Caroline cried out. I listened for any feet on the deck but it was completely silent. The boat rocked violently side to side and soon, I found my own feet in a little layer of water. Assuming it was just a collection of rain water, we all stood around the cabin and tried to get back to what we were doing. Just then, a tremendous boom came from below that had us trembling. Colby, being a hero, rushed out of the cabin, but came back only a minute later, coughing.

"The pipes burst with water everywhere! Plus there's smoke coming out of the engine!" He shouted at us. We all were frozen in shock. A huge wave hit the boat, making us tumble into each other. Was anyone steering the boat?! That was not good. The rain was slamming the side of the boat, or was that the waves? Just looking into everyone else's eyes said exactly what I was thinking. We were going to sink. With Bethany leading the way, we raced onto the slippery, smoke and water covered empty deck to find the three life boats missing. All that was left was a small orange rubber raft.

"They left without us!" Emilia cried against the howling wind. Without even thinking, we piled into the cramped raft. We just fit and I was crammed between Nick and Emilia. Calvin realized the raft from its holding spot on the deck and we plummeted down to the water that was dangerously close to the boat. Bidziil and Calvin grabbed the oars and started rowing us away. It felt as though it was some scene from *Titanic* but it was actually really happening. I looked back at the sinking ship and saw the light of our cabin. A pang hit my chest. I just realized that

I had left my only picture of my mom inside my duffle bag. The top of the boat hit the water with a suction cup sound and everything went back. Lightning lit up the sky to reveal an empty ocean. That's when I leaned over the side of the boat and threw up.

After I finished throwing up the dinner we had, I recalled hands holding my hair back. I turned from the edge of the raft and saw Nick holding my hair. He smiled sheepishly.

"Are you done?" He asked, letting go.

"Yes," I managed to squeak out. One glance around the tiny raft told me that Nick and I were the only ones awake. Everyone else was collapsed on the floor and the boys were snoring. "What happened?"

"Everyone passed out around hour three. I can't believe the crew deserted us," Nick whispered, careful not to wake anyone. My stomach churned again. Hour three. Crew deserted. How could they? Diane was so nice to us! Nick caught my hair just as I threw up over the side of the raft again.

"I'm sorry. I thought I was done," I turned back to him.

"It's okay. You have soft hair," Nick said to me. I blinked in surprise.

"Thanks. No one had ever really complimented me before," I coughed and leaned against the side of the raft. His eyebrows shot up.

"Really?" He asked slightly smiling, "I'm glad I could be the first." A row of pearly teeth appeared from this action. I go for guys with good teeth. But, I would only date him if his awful haircut grew out. Wait, I couldn't think of romance at this time! We were castaways at sea!

23

"Nick, how long have we been out here?" I asked, realizing I was throwing up/leaning against the side of the boat for a long time.

"About six hours," He said glancing at his conveniently waterproof watch.

"Six hours!" I shot straight up. Earlier that night, Diane said that we would hit our next island, the first of five islands all in a row, in about three hours. "Nick, did you happen to see land anytime?" He just looked at me.

"If I saw land, we'd be there by now," He crossed his arms and lied down, obviously hurt by my accusation. Of course if he saw land he would have done everything he could to get us there.

"Diane said that we were three hours away from islands before we sank. If we are six hours away from when we sank then," I couldn't finish my sentence, but Nick could.

"Then we went in the opposite direction then the boat was headed for and probably where the crew went. We went out into open water," Nick gulped loudly. The *Lost* theme song began playing in my head. We were really, truly lost. It was no TV show; it was the no reality thing where we would get money in the end. It was the real deal.

"I wish I never agreed to go on this stupid trip," I mumbled to myself. Nick seemed to have heard be because he said,

"At least *you* had a choice," I stared into his vibrant eyes.

"No. I didn't. And if you think I did, then you're seriously mistaken," I spat. I didn't care if I sounded exasperated. I was. I was furious at the crew for doing this to us, my dad putting me on that cursed boat and at my mother for leaving me. I know she didn't have a choice; it wasn't her decision, but if she hadn't hit the gas so hard that night, she might have been there right now, and I would have been with her.

"Why would the crew leave us to go down with the ship?" Nick wondered out loud. His voice cut through the still air, making him sound like he was ten years old.

"I have no idea," I groaned and buried my head in my hands so he wouldn't see me cry. He must have heard me though because he attempted to shift his body to put his outstretched arm around me. But as he did, the boat rocked and dipped into the water, letting in only a little bit of the salty ocean. But it was enough to wake everyone up and have them complain about the water that filled their shoes. A wave jostled our little life boat and suddenly I felt something hit against it. Obviously everyone else had felt it too because we all looked at one another and fell dead silent. Colby slowly leaned over the side, only to reel back shortly after.

"Well, let's just say we're not alone," he quivered.

"What do you mean?" I asked, knowing exactly what he was talking about.

"We're um, surrounded by sharks," He whispered, scratching his head as if saying the name of the animal would cause it to attack. It was Bethany's scream that broke the tense silence.

"Sharks! They are seriously going to mess up my hair!" She clasped her hands atop her head and I rolled my eyes.

25

"Bethany, if you get in the water with the sharks, or they tear the raft to shreds, you're not going to be worrying about a bad hair day," I pointed out. I wasn't an expert, but I thought circling sharks usually meant that they were hungry.

"Plus, your hair is already messy," Caroline laughed. It was true. Her blonde hair was tied together in huge knots, giving off the illusion that she had gigantic messy curls. Bidzill snorted at Caroline's comment while Colby reached across and tried to untangle her hair.

"We have bigger problems then hair!" I snapped. Those sharks were circling us and our boat wasn't very strong. Instantly, I had an idea. I grabbed one of the oars that was attached to the side of the raft and leaned over, waiting for one to circle. Soon enough, just as its ugly snout rounded the edge, I smacked my oar on top of its nose as hard as I could without falling out of the raft.

"Uh, Monica what are you doing?" Emilia asked, rubbing her eyes.

"I saw on Animal Planet once that if you smacked sharks on their snouts, they let go of whatever they were holding. I'm just hoping that they'll swim away," I explained and smacked another one. So far it was working. I grabbed the other oar and tossed it to Calvin who was on the other side of the boat.

"What attracted the sharks in the first place?" Bidziil questioned, "sharks just don't circle a boat for no reason." He had a point. We all scanned each other and the boat looking for any signs of food or blood. That's when Calvin smacked a shark, revealing his back to us. His blue shirt was torn and where the skin was exposed was raw and dripping slowly with blood. The blood was spilling down his back and over the side of the boat. Nick spotted it the same time I did.

"Calvin! It's you the sharks are after. You're bleeding," He climbed across everyone and pulled Calvin away from the edge. Then he forced him to lie down on his stomach.

"How am I bleeding? I don't remember cutting myself. And why is it on my back?" Calvin asked mostly to himself. His brown eyes were frantic and his back muscles: bulging. I glanced at Caroline who was just as fixated on them as I was.

"How should I know?" Nick asked, tearing off a piece of Calvin's shirt to wrap around the wound. Meanwhile, Bidziil used the oar to smack on of the lingering sharks.

"Oh I remember. The rope that held our boat hit his back when we plunged into the water. It must have burned him so much that he started bleeding," Caroline put one finger to her lips as she recalled.

"Huh. I didn't even feel that," Calvin said, amazed.

"Nick? How did you learn to bandage wounds and stuff?" I asked, cocking an eyebrow. Nick didn't even bother looking up as he answered.

"I was the first one in my Boy Scouts troupe to get the First Aid badge." I laughed inwardly. Boy Scout. Lame. He caught my smirk.

"What? You think that it's funny that Calvin's hurt and we are miles away from any island?" He gestured rapidly at the ocean. Calvin sat up and inched towards the center of the boat.

"No. I find it funny that you were a Boy Scout," I giggled. He huffed.

"Fine. Find it funny. I don't care. But it might come in handy some day," he said and turned to the water.

"Well! That's the last of them!" Bidziil announced and put the oar back on the side of the boat. Nobody spoke for a while and soon the waves drifted me off to sleep.

When I awoke only a couple of hours later, everything was exactly the same. We were still drifting in the ocean, we were still castaways and we were still cranky. The only thing that changed was that I was even more hungry and thirsty than I was before and the sky was getting a little bit lighter. I sat up in the raft and looked around. You would have thought we were all stars in a horror movie. Bethany's hair was messier than ever, Calvin's back was grosser and Colby, well, he actually looked even better than before. Must have been all the ruggedness.

"We're all going to die," Bethany moaned. The rest of us groaned and someone said "shut up". I couldn't tell who it was.

"We will if we aren't rescued soon," I found myself saying. Seven pairs of eyes shot daggers at me.

"Okay we can't talk like that! Either we'll get rescued or we'll find land," Nick said, trying to lift everyone's sprits. So far it wasn't working. We drifted in silence for what seemed like hours. We were hungry and thirsty and the sun was beating right on us. At around what seemed like mid day, clouds drifted in front of the sun. We all breathed a sigh of relief. But then it began to rain. We all groaned.

"Seriously? Are we ever going to get a break?" Caroline yelled up to the sky. The clouds answered with more rain.

"Hey guys, um, I'm sitting in a puddle," Colby yelled over the noise of rain hitting the ocean. Colby was right. There was a thin layer of water collecting. Quickly, we all cupped our hands and started tossing water out of the boat.

"Wait!" Nick shouted after thirty seconds. He reached down with his cupped hands and began to drink the water. I followed. I never thought water could taste so good. It was like my taste buds were exploding with gratitude.

"It won't last long. We need to drink as much as we can," Nick instructed and I gulp the water harder. The rain suddenly cut off and soon I was sucking the bottom of the boat.

"Now what do we do?" Bethany whined.

"We wait," Calvin said quietly. And we did.

The sun was only a little lower in the sky when Nick suddenly shot up, rocking to boat.

"Look!" he shouted and pointed in the direction behind me. The rainstorm left a foggy mist over the ocean and looming out in the distance was a faded black silhouette of an island. A mountain peak was at the top with thick green forests surrounding it, giving it the classic deserted island feel. We stared at the island for a good three minutes, our thoughts on land, rescue and hope.

"Do you know," Caroline started.

"Dry land," Emilia breathed.

"Food," Calvin sighed in a shaky voice.

"Rescue," I managed.

"Shelter," Nick stuttered.

"Some place to go to the bathroom," Colby blurted.

"Wild animals," Bidziil whispered.

"Hairdryer," Sighed Bethany in a sickening loving voice. We all turned to stare at her, even Colby.

"What? There's not going to be a five star resort?" Clearly she did not get the whole deserted island thing. Idiot. The island was still miles away and I fumbled to get something to move the boat along with. Finally, I found the oars, lying across the floor. I tossed one to Caroline and we started rowing. Now, to be honest, moving a boat full of teenagers was not as easy as it sounded. Turns out, it could get pretty heavy and tiring. Only after fifteen minutes, we were guessing we were still about two miles away but Caroline and I were so tired, we couldn't row anymore. Bidziil and Nick took over but proved that they weren't any better than us. Finally we persuaded Calvin and Colby to give it a shot. With Calvin and Colby's muscles, maybe we could have made it ashore.

The sun was slightly lower in the sky, already streaked with pink, and we were all soaked in sea water and sweat by the time the water was shallow enough to pull the raft in. I jumped out to help Emilia and Nick pull the boat out of the water and up onto the beach.

"Land!" Screamed Bethany and she began kissing the sand. She soon realized that sand does not taste that great and started spitting it out. I laid my wet body against the rough but smooth texture of the sand, realizing that we were alone. All alone. Eight teenagers, alone on an island.

"Well, I guess we have to set up camp," Nick took charge. I was way too tired to think about anything else but cool refreshing water to drink.

"You know what, we need water first, then we can get enough energy to set up camp," I suggested, gently pealing myself off the ground.

"Good idea. Monica you and Bethany go look for water. Colby and Bidziil can look for usable sticks or logs for firewood, Caroline and Emilia can take a walk to find out how long this beach goes on for, and Calvin and I will go hunting," Nick stood with his hands on his hips, clearly proud of what he just accomplished.

"Who made you boss?" I asked, cocking my head. Shouldn't we vote or something for leader? I would vote for Bidziil. He seemed sensible enough.

"Me that's who. It's obvious that no one else is going to take charge so why not me?" I shook my head. He may have had some Boy Scout experience but he wasn't with a troupe and that wasn't going to help too much out there in the wild.

"Yeah sure, go be the bossy one but don't com crying to me when it doesn't work out," I didn't want to be blamed for controlling other people's lives. That's why I never ran for student body president back in school. Nick stared at me in a way that I remember only seeing once. But instead of kissing me like Riley used to do, he just grunted and walked off. I didn't want him to kiss me anyway. Well, okay, there was that certain butterfly feeling but only for two seconds. Like I said, it was no time for romance. I glared at his back and then turned to Bethany.

"Come on Bethany, I'm thirsty," I pulled her to her feet, dragging her behind me as I pushed my way through the woods, ignoring the voice coming from the beach that said:

"Oooh, tension already. This is going to be exciting." I couldn't tell who it was, but it sounded suspiciously like Colby.

"Why do I have to go with you?" Bethany whined. I crossed my sore arms and rolled my yes. She continued complaining about the stupidest little things like bugs and I finally snapped. I stopped midstride and turned my body to face her twig thin image.

"Look. I don't want to be here either you know. But we have to. We didn't have a choice whether or not we wanted to live off this island but hey, we have to deal with it which means you do too," feeling proud of myself, I walked on ahead, hearing the distant murmuring of a stream.

Pushing past the trees, a small creek bubbled along uneven rocks that looked untouched. I kneeled down and dipped my hands into the cool fresh water. Because I was so immersed in the stream, I didn't notice when Bethany emerged from the trees and stepped beside me. The water was so close to the beach! Bethany's voice made me jump.

"How are we going to get the water back to the beach?" She asked, stepping closer to the water. I stood up and wiped my mouth on my hand and turned to face her.

"We should tell the rest of the group first and then we can figure it out," I suggested and glanced around. I wasn't as mesmerized with the stream now, but more with the beauty of the place. I realized that it was more of a cove. To my left was the beginning of the lush mountain that had a gorgeous waterfall feeding into a crystal clear pool that trickled into the stream. The stream continued above the waterfall and a cliff was hanging out above the pool almost like a diving board. It was truly stunning.

"Fine," Bethany huffed and flipped her hair. We began walking back towards the faint line of beach in front of us. It's amazing how obnoxious she is. When we pushed through the last of the trees and step onto the soft sand, it turned out that only Colby and Bidziil were back.

Hey, we found a stream. Well actually it's a cove at the base of the mountain that has a fresh water stream and pool," I sat down on the sand and leaned back against my arms, closing my eyes against the sun.

"That's great! But how will we get the water back to camp?" Bidziil questioned as he broke long braches in two.

"Could we use the two pitchers that I found in that bag?" Colby pointed to a faded and very wet first aid kit with eh symbol of the Red Cross on it. I stared at it dumbfounded.

"Colby, where did you find that? I didn't see anything like this when I looked," I pointed out. Colby ran a hand through his tangled hair and blushed a soft pink. I felt myself swoon. Blushing made him look hotter than he already was. My heart was fluttering so fast I was afraid it would sprout wings and fly away.

"I um, used it as a pillow," Colby confessed and began putting the broken sticks into a pile. I glanced at Bidziil. He just shrugged before I opened the kit. I pulled out two thermoses that were the farthest thing from pitchers. I also pulled out a pack of matches that I tossed to Bidziil. Just then, Nick and Calvin entered our little campsite with only coconuts in their hands.

"Well we know one thing's for sure. This is definitely a tropical island," Calvin laughed and placed the coconuts next to Colby on the sand.

"How did you get those out of a tree? Aren't they like really really high?" Bethany asked, making her annoying presence known.

"We gathered the ones that had already fallen from the tree," Nick answered her as he emptied his armload next to Calvin's. Taking the end of his shirt, he wiped the sweat off his forehead. The day was getting hot fast.

"Hey did you find fresh water?" Nick asked me, our previous tension forgotten. I stood up and tossed him one of the thermoses.

"Yup, here, you're coming with me this time," I stared walking in the direction of the stream. My shorts caught on a bush but I didn't stop to unhook them and just let the bush tear off a piece of fabric. All our clothes were ruined already. If it wasn't the salt water that did them in then it was the sand. I thought to myself before we know it we'll have to make our clothes out of palm leaves. Sweat beads were starting to form on my forehead, making me rush for the pool. It wasn't normal heat; it was like we were on a cookie that was burning in the oven for too long.

When we reached the stream and the pool, Nick became fascinated.

"Wow," He said and then kneeled down by the stream as I had done earlier. My thoughts flashed to the pool at my school back home. I am on the dive team there and am the best high diver there is in our town. Nothing beats the thrill of stepping up to the edge, toes wiggling off the side and the crowd cheering your name. the bounce of the board, the rush of wind as you take your dive or the silent splash as you hit the smooth water. Nothing beats that. My mind reluctantly drags back to reality when I hear Nick sigh.

"This place is incredible," he was gazing all around like some tourist who was in Europe for the first time. Nick continued to cup his hands and gulp the water. I kneeled beside him and hand him one of the thermoses.

"Oh, right," Nick gulped and filled his thermos.

"You know, this could be our place," He said glancing quickly at me. I snorted and blushed. Then we both burst out laughing.

"Yeah, ok, we can't just not tell everybody about this place. Besides Bethany already knows about it and it's too close to camp," I made excuses while wiping my eyes free of tears. The idea of having a place with Nick frightened me a little and I had no idea why. Sure, he was cute in his own way, but very nerdy at the same time. So not my type. But then, why did I feel kind of drawn to him?

"That cliff looked good for diving, you want to try?" Nick read my mind. The water was deep, but not so deep that you couldn't see the bottom. No fish swam in the glass like pool and the cliff hung just above the water, the perfect height for any kind of dive. I grin mischievously.

"Race you to the top!" I shouted and bolted ahead before he could register what just happened.

"No fair!" I heard him call from not far behind. Luckily, all of us had bathing suits on under our clothes that we put on for the islands we were supposed to see on the cruise. Of course, that was before the storm and now we were using them like they were our underwear. I know, gross. I reached the top and stripped off my sweaty shorts, sneakers and shirt. Nick made it up just in time to see me take off my shirt. I caught him eyeing my chest. I'm not huge in that department but enough that I could easily attract guys. If I wanted to. Which I don't.

"Hey keep your eyes to yourself," I snapped and folded my arms across my chest. He blushed crimson. Normally, I wear a one-piece bathing suit for swimming, but I accidentally grabbed the one bikini a brought on this trip instead. Now, I had no choice but to show off my body, which is good I guess. It's not like I have a bad body or anything, but I just don't like to flounce what I don't have to. Oh god I'm babbling. Nick took off his shorts and t-shirt revealing swim trunks underneath. I straightened my ponytail and put my back to the edge.

"Push me," I demanded. For some reason, I felt the need to show off in front of Nick, but he just looked at me like I was. Hey, after all that time on the ocean maybe I am.

"You want me to do what?" He crossed his arms in front of his hidden, but there, six pack.

"Just lightly push me," I said again. He raised one of his eyebrows but did as he was told. His touch on my shoulder sent ice cold shivers up my spine but I didn't flinch. Instead, I curved my back and used the push to propel myself off the edge, into a perfect backwards dive. My hands sliced the cool pool which refreshed my warm body. The dive drove me through the water and soon I forced my way to the top just as Nick did a large cannonball. Nick emerged from the depths laughing as he slicked back his short black hair.

"What was that?" I laughed.

"A super cannonball! I could never do a dive like you did. Let me guess, dive team?" I nodded and splashed him.

"Hey, this is a no splashing zone," he mimicked a life guard's voice, causing me to splash him again. Then he stopped.

"You know, we can't just refill the thermoses every time someone wants a drink," Nick floated on his back but used his arms to swim towards the bank of the stream. HE picked up a thermos and turned it over and over in his hands. Suddenly, Caroline came running the rough the trees, holding up a jug.

"Hey love birds! Look what I found in the bag!" She exclaimed.

"We are not love birds," I defended as I climbed out of the pool and pulled on my clothes. Nick did the same and soon we filled the jugs and thermoses with water and headed back to camp.

"What bag?" Nick finally asks.

"Colby used a first aid bag as a pillow and we just opened it," I explained and fight through the last few trees to the beach. Emilia, Colby, Calvin and Bethany were huddled around a small fire going through the first aid bag while Bidziil was spelling something in the sand with sticks. I glanced at Bidziil and realized that he was spelling out the word Help. Figuring he got it under control, I take a seat next to Emilia in the sand. The first aid bag seemed more like a survival bag when I pulled out the hatchet.

"Where are we going to sleep tonight?" Emilia asked in a frightened tone, "and I'm so hungry."

"Here, eat a coconut," Nick passes one of the fruit that he just cut open with the hatchet, "We can use the raft for now, and tomorrow we can use the hatchet to build shelter," Nick answered Emilia's question and pulled the raft higher up onto the beach and tied it to a tree. The tide was getting dangerously close to our campsite and the beach wasn't that wide. The sky was getting darker and it doesn't seem real that we had already spent an entire day on the island. My stomach rumbled as Nick used the hatchet to crack open the rest of the coconuts. I drank the sweet milk and eat the fruit. And then, I stopped chewing. The sun went down, leaving the dim light of our campfire as our only light. But that wasn't what was bothering me. My feet felt wet against my sneakers and I looked down to see that the tide had risen to where we were and was slowing putting our fire out. Calvin and Bidziil jumped up and tie the ropes that were holding the raft tighter. It was soon floating and we all piled into the raft to sleep. Darkness engulfed us and I settled against the side feeling the raft rock in the shallow water. The sticks used the write HELP floated by and it seemed to take its friend hope with it. If the tide covered the beach every night, we had to build our camp and shelter near the pool. As I rolled over, I recalled something my mother always told me before I went to bed. Tomorrow is a new day.

CHAPTER 4: 2 DAYS AFTER SHIPWRECK

The next morning, I awoke to the blinding sun in my eyes and the nasty taste of morning breath in my mouth. I stretched, working all the kinks out of my back and surveyed the scene. By the look of it, only Colby, Calvin and I were up. I swung my sunburned tired legs over the side of the raft onto freshly wet sand. The salt water smell filled the air and I breathed in a lung full. Before I went on the trip, I loved the smell. After spending so much time out on the water in the past couple days, I'd grown to loathe it.

While the sand squished between my toes, I stumbled over to the campfire. Talking softly, the boys were huddled around the glow, cooking a fish.

"Where'd you get the fish?" I asked while finger combing my tousled hair. Giving up, I pulled it into a ponytail.

"I speared it," Calvin boasted, holding up a long stick that was shaped into the form of a spear. On the side with the ragged point, a small but fat fish hang, the point covered in dried blood. Calvin had done a nice job scaling, but the sight of the dead fish still made me shudder.

"So we all know that we can't keep our camp here at high tide," I started and plopped down onto the sand, leaning back on my hands.

"Right, but where else are we going to go?" Colby asked, rotating the fish over the fire.

"Well, we know that we need fresh water, and that we don't have much to hold the water in right?" I dragged my suggestion out, hoping it would seem more dramatic than it actually was. Colby and Calvin nodded in sync.

"So why don't we move our camp to the pool? It's fresh water, clean enough to bathe in and the clearing is big enough to build a hut or something," I concluded, feeling satisfied with myself. The guys shared a glance.

"How long do you expect us to be here? A ship is probably going to come at any moment and because we move our came to that little pool, they won't see us," Calvin pointed out.

"Calvin think about it, a ship wouldn't be able to see us without a signal fire of some sort and we can build that at the camp near the pool," I argued.

"She's right dude, plus it would be nice to go swimming," Colby wiggled his eyebrows. It was kind of immature but just hearing him say that I was right sent shivers up and down my spine and made me pulse with energy to kiss him. Although, I don't think he would have acted well if I just tackled him with kisses right then and there.

"Why don't we go check it out and make sure that I *am* right," I offered, standing up and brushing off the caked sand on my shorts.

"You two go, I'll stay here in case the others wake up and wonder where everyone went," Calvin suggested, taking the fish from Colby's hands.

"Okay," Colby shrugged and put his hand on the small of my back, "Lead the way Monica." I stumbled through the trees,

41

very aware of Colby's touch. Reaching the pool, I spread out my arms, indicating the clearing that we were standing in. Colby surveyed the clearing and nodded his blonde head.

"This could work. You were definitely right," He said approving. He said it again. I was right. Tingles descended throughout my body.

"You know, this could be our place," he said suggestively. Something in his voice made me feel betrayal to Nick. He said the same thing and suddenly, I wanted Nick's and my place to be real.

"We can't have a place, everyone's going to be using it if we build the camp here," I pointed our hurriedly.

"Fine," Colby muttered so low I almost couldn't hear it. He knelt by the water and took a drink out of his cupped hands. When Colby stood up from his crouched position and started coming towards me, my lips quiver in anticipation. Fantasies of what he was going to say or do were running through my head.

"I'm sorry about that night we met on the deck, I didn't mean to act like I didn't care, it's just that I've never known someone who lost a parent and I didn't really know what to say," He inched closer enough that I could see brown flecks in his green eyes. That stare. The same one Riley used to give me and the one Nick gave me yesterday. This stare is closer to Riley's though and it was a little more intense. Just as Colby's mouth slowly inched towards mine, a crack of a twig made us jump at least ten feet apart from each other. Bethany and Emilia stepped out from the forest, the others following closely behind.

"Colby I was looking all over for you!" Bethany said in a sing-song voice. Colby caught up to her like a love sick puppy and together they began walking towards the diving rock. It made me sick. Just moments ago I was sure he was going to kiss me and then he went off with Bethany.

"Wow Nick, you were right, this place does work for our campsite," Bidziil said, gazing around. Fury bubbled up inside. Nick was right?

"Wait a minute. Nick was right? This was my idea!" I shouted and pointed at my chest. I hate it when I'm not heard. It's happened too many times in my life and now that we were stranded on an island, it was not going to happen here. Nick calmly made his way towards me.

"It was both our ideas. You found this place and we both had the campsite idea. I was trying to tell you it yesterday before we got interrupted by Caroline. You just beat me to it to tell everyone," Nick reasoned. My fury was quickly replaced by embarrassment.

"Oh yeah," I chocked dumbly. *Now* I remembered our conversation about thermoses.

"Can we swim in the water?" Emilia asked. Without waiting for an answer, everyone but Nick and I jumped into the mirror like pool.

"I liked swimming in the pool better than the ocean back home. Maybe the ocean here is different. It's probably warmer," I attempted conversation.

"Mmhmm," mumbled Nick, half listening.

"Nick what are you doing?" I asked as he began gathering twigs.

"I think we should lay out where our huts should be," He suggested, mapping out a rather small square with the twigs. I hovered over his shoulder as he laid out some twigs in a small circle.

"What's that supposed to be?" I asked. Why would we need a small circle inside a small square out here in the jungle? It wasn't Geometry class.

"This will be the outhouse. Basically the hole is where you, you know, and the square will be where you walk in," He explained, pointing with a stick/

"Well, then the square needs to be bigger. I can barely fit in it," I demonstrated by stepping into the square with my size seven feet and my toes touched the side of the square. My sneakers broke most of the little twigs for the whole.

"Oh I see. Yeah that might help," Nick blushed and started widening the sides.

"Much better," I said and now I could actually fit my whole feet inside the square. I called everyone out of the water so we could actually have a place to sleep tonight if we hurry. I copied what Nick was doing and began gathering more sticks to outline the huts. Luckily this was a jungle and there were sticks everywhere. It was a good thing we weren't stranded in some weird place like the Sahara desert.

Before long, the plans were done. We had an outhouse, a place for the fire pit, a girl's hut, a boy's hut and a "living room" hut.

"Now what do we make the walls out of?" Nick asked himself, rubbing his chin. For some strange reason, his simple

44

action sent as much shivers down my spine as Colby's comment did.

"You didn't think of that before?" I ran my dirty hand through my hair, not even caring how it would make it look.

"Well, no actually. Maybe we can weave together some vines. The walls can go halfway up for privacy and so you can still get a nice breeze." While the others got busy again on the huts, Caroline and I walked off in search of some vines.

"How are we supposed to weave the vines?" She asked as we made our way through the dense jungle. A monkey screeched in front of us as it swung in the trees.

"Nick said he'll show us. Maybe they'll be thin," I hoped. It would be really hard to weave thick vines. Finally, we came across some low hanging vies over a tiny tidal pool that held one small crab.

"How did a tidal pool get all the way up here? The beach is almost a mile that way," Caroline thrust a hand in the direction we had just come from.

"An underground spring? I shrugged. Caroline tugged on one of the vines and found that it came off the tree pretty easily. I did the same and tug on more.

"Let's gather up as many as we can carry. That way we don't have to come back for more," She suggested and began pulling down more vines. We pulled down vines until our arms were weighed with them.

"Okay I think that's enough, let's head back to camp," I panted and began leading the way.

Our journey back to camp felt twice as long. Caroline fell twice and I had to drop my vines to help her pick up hers. Exhausted and covered in thick mud, we finally made it back to camp.

"Sheesh. What happened to you guys? You look like you were hit by a football team," Calvin commented. Even a not so nice comment sounded good in his southern accent. Calvin and Colby were in the middle of putting long bamboo sticks into the ground. I had a feeling they were for the roof.

"We got the vines. It was tough carrying them back. Now how are we going to tie them?" I asked and set my pile on top of Caroline's already dropped pile.

"You have to weave them. Here let me show you," Nick came over and took four vines. He laid them parallel to each to each other and then grabbed another vine.

"You have to weave in, then out, in, then out," He demonstrated, moving his vine through the four others and pulling tight.

"See, this will be the height and length of one wall of the outhouse. Keep doing it with the vines and I'll show Bidziil, Bethany and Emilia how to do it. Colby and Calvin can keep working on the roof poles," Nick instructed. I was right, the bamboo sticks were going to be used to hold up the roof.

Before long, the five of us were weaving at a fast pace, already had made all the walls for the outhouse and girls hut. I wiped the sweat off my brown and realized the sun was setting.

"Maybe we should stop for today, we have enough room in the girls hut for all of us," I suggested. My stomach grumbled, reminding me that we had other stuff we needed to get done.

"We need food," I groaned, standing up from my sitting position.

"That would sure help. Hey guys, why don't we go get the fish and you can start building the fire," Bidziil suggested to us, already headed towards the beach. The fishing pole that he made this morning was in his tan hand. Nick, Colby and Calvin followed, each carrying their own fishing pole. I had no idea when they had time to make those.

"So. How should we start this fire?" Emilia asked, brushing dirt off her skirt.

"I'll get the firewood," Caroline suggested and headed to our wood pile by the boy's hut.

"I'll get the bag," I said and headed over to our survival bag. Yesterday, the boys found a lighter we could use to get a fire started in there. I picked up the tiny lighter and headed back to Caroline's wood pile. Soon, the fire was going and the night had turned an inky black. The full moon reflected on the pool, tempting me to take a dip in it.

"How about a late night swim?" I teased and got to my feet.

"We could all use a bath," Caroline shrugged, already taking off her shorts.

"I agree but the boys have been gone a long time. What if they come back when we're in there?" Emilia timidly asked.

"We're keeping our bathing suits on. We're definitely not skinny dipping," Bethany said, the fire light glistening on her face as she stripped of her clothes.

"Last one in has to eat fish skin!" I yelled and took off running into the water. The warmness engulfed me instantly. It wrapped its warm temperature around me like a mother's hug. A mother's hug that I hadn't felt in a long time. The temperature was a dramatic difference in temperature compared to the heat today. I guessed the water must have been about eighty degrees which made today about ninety five. Splashes of water sounded and then three heads popped out of the water. After about twenty minutes and another dunk underwater, I scampered out of the pool, brushing my wet hair off my forehead. My body felt slightly cooler after my evening swim. Pulling my clothes over top of my bathing suit, I wrung out my hair and pulled on my flip flops and headed towards the beach. My grumbling stomach seemed to have a mind of its own.

"Dude this is the biggest yet!" Colby's chuckle floated up from the beach. I stuck my hands in my shorts pockets and emerged from the trees.

"I don't think that's a fish," I heard Nick say. Quietly coming up behind them, I leaned over their shoulders and gasped.

"That's my bag!" I shouted, forgetting that I was close to their ears.

"Ahhh!" The guys screamed and leaped away from me. Bidziil actually jumped into Calvin's arms, shrieking like a girl. I began laughing so hard that it took several minutes for me to completely stop and even then I was wiping away laughter tears. They weren't going to hear the end of this. I pushed my hysterical thoughts aside and turned to my duffle bag that lay on the beach covered in sand and seaweed. I picked up the waterlogged strap and put it over my shoulder.

"Do we have enough fish for us to eat tonight? You guys were out here for a long time," I asked and switched the strap to my other shoulder. The bag's weight was heavy with water. Calvin turned to the pile of at least five fish that they've caught.

"We had a little trouble with the line first, then when we did catch a fish we tossed it back out hoping to get a bigger fish. But when we pulled it back, only the head was still intact. It took a lot of effort to get these fish," Calvin explained.

"Well I think we're having a feast tonight," Bidziil grinned. I headed towards the glowing light in the distance and the giggles that wafted into the night. Coming into the clearing I set my duffle bag on the ground and immediately the girls crowded around it.

"What is that?" Caroline asked, crouching next to my bag.

"It's my duffle bag that I never really unpacked. It just washed up on the beach," I said, also crouching.

"Actually, Colby caught it with a fishing hook," Nick corrected. I raised my eyebrows at Colby and then slowly but firmly unzipped my bag.

CHAPTER 5: 2 DAYS AFTER SHIPWRECK

The first thing I saw was my uneaten granola bar. Unharmed and still wrapped.

"Give me!" Bethany shouted, making a mad grab for the delicious chocolate covered bar.

"Beth we have to share!" I yelled over her struggles, clutching the granola bar to my chest.

"I thought I told you never to call me that!" She bellowed. Oops. My mistake. Oh well *Bethany*, deal with it. I ignored her as she stomped away and tossed Bidziil the granola bar.

"Could you cut that into eight pieces?" I asked him. I was tempted to say seven. Bidziil nodded, his eyes growing huge. I could practically see his mouth watering. He wondered off in search for a knife in the survival bag. The next item I pulled out of my bag was one of my favorite t-shirts. I was saving it for the day we were supposed to go up in a helicopter.

"We can share this," I handed it to Caroline. I then pulled out a pair of flip flops and a pair of sweats. I handed those to Caroline as well. That was it for the clothes sadly. I now recalled that I had unpacked everything else into the drawers I was given on the ship. Out of the bag next was an umbrella I packed in there in case it rained. It never did.

"That would be perfect for shade," Nick commented. I tossed it to him. The next and last two things I pulled out surprised me the most. The picture of my mother and my last letter from Riley.

"These are private," I mumbled and headed towards a palm tree at the edge of the fire light glow. There, I sat and opened the letter that I already knew backwards and forwards.

Dear Monica,

I know that this is selfish of me to tell you this by letter. I just seemed like the best way to end our "thing". If that's what you would call it. And, I just can't tell you this in person. I love you Monica and I always will. But I don't think we should see each other anymore. I'm sorry that your mother passed away, I truly am, but you're always depressed now when you're with me. I see you having fun with your friends and I don't get why you're not like that with me. I need to have fun with someone and that someone is not you. (Maybe Emily Cox though). I truly am sorry.

Please forgive me,

RILEY

Tears were making it hard to read the worn piece of paper. I missed the way he would sign his name in all caps. Instantly my mind transported me to someplace else. I was standing by my beat up locker freshman year. Kayce was standing next to me chatting about something I had absolutely no interest in. I turned my head to see if Rachel was coming down the hall and that's when I first saw him. It was a total slow motion moment. Riley was walking down the hall, laughing with some guys who were wearing basketball jerseys. I could feel that my mouth was wide open and Kayce stopped talking to see what I was gaping at.

"Who is that?" I managed to whisper just as Riley caught my eye. He smiled.

"That's Riley St. Bridges, the new student. I think he just moved here from Texas. He's a sophomore," Kayce explained. My eyes stayed on him for another full minute before he came over. I remember he said hi and Kayce said bye.

"So are you okay? You had this far off look on your face," Riley had said. I nodded, a blush creeping across my cheeks.

"I thought it was cute. Do you want to go out sometime?" offered Riley. He was forward and I had liked that. I had just nodded. We dated for a while after that. It was only a couple months before my mother died. But he was right. Letter writing *was* our thing. We would write notes to each other whenever we weren't together. He was also right again. I did become depressed with him after my mother died. I was upset that my mother never had a guy as nice as Riley. It wasn't fair that I got one and she didn't. Riley and I still went out for another couple months. Then just days before our one year anniversary, I guess he just had enough. We had written letter but his were detailed and mine were almost always one worded. I remember that after I got this letter, I knew I was never going to be like my mother and settle for someone who abused me. I wasn't going to make her bad choice. I was me and I wanted Riley. But it was too late.

Fresh tears spilled over when I flipped over the picture of my mom. Some people say she looks like me, but honestly I don't see much of a resemblance. Sure, we have the same nose and the same eyes but other than that, I was all my dad. Something I wished I could change.

"Hey are you okay?" Colby asked, coming to sit next to me.

"Yeah I'm fine. Just happy about seeing my stuff," I fibbed. Colby nodded but I could tell he knew I was lying.

"Okay. Fish is ready," He said before walking back towards the fire. I stared at the picture of my mom for a long time after that, long after the last fish was eaten. I didn't care. I wasn't hungry anymore. My mother looked so beautiful in that photograph. It was taken the summer before she died when she and I went to visit my Aunt in Florida. The three of us were carefree. In the photo, her head was tilted back and she was laughing. The sun was glimmering off her dark blonde hair, turning it to pure honey.

"Do you want something to eat? I saved you a plate," Nick asked as he sat next to me, a piece of fish on top of our makeshift plates. Really they were just leaves. I hadn't even heard him approach.

"Not really," I sniffed and wiped my tire eyes.

"You okay? Colby told everyone that you were okay but you don't look it," He set the fish down and looked over my shoulder to see what I was staring at.

"Is that your mom?" He asked, his breath close to my ear. Despite my emotions, I still got warm chills. I sniffed again.

"Yeah. She, um, died in a car accident when I was fifteen," I looked at the sand, careful to keep my tear stained eyes from him.

"God, I'm so sorry," Nick said softly and put a comforting arm around me. Suddenly, at his touch, I found myself telling him everything. My dad abusing my mother, my mom's frantic getaway and her death. I even told him about Riley. I didn't feel vulnerable like I did with Colby. I needed to open up to Nick. There was something about him that I knew he would listen to me. I lifted my head and realized we were sitting in the dark.

"I need to go to sleep," I stood up and stretched, my back aching from leaning against the tree.

"Then let's go. And Monica?" I turned towards him. He reached out a calloused hand and rested it on mine.

"I really am sorry that you had to go through all that," His eyes had a watery tinge to them that set me on edge. I nodded and lead the way towards the huts.

The girls hut was crowded but there was just enough room for Nick and me. I crawled over to the space between the wall and Caroline while Nick took the space next to the wall and Calvin. For some weird reason, all of us were sleeping in a row, like pigs in a blanket. Well, except for the blanket. It was warm enough to sleep without anything on top of me. But as I turned to face the wall, I heard the distant rumbling of thunder and shivered. There was never another time when I wished desperately to have Nick by my side.

I awoke in the middle of the night to the soft sound of rain on the roof. Rubbing my eyes, I sat up and adjusted to the darkness. Everyone was up and huddled against the far walls where we put up our roof. We didn't have enough material to finish the middle yet. I inched to the wall next to Emilia just as the first sheet of rain pounded the Earth. It soon became clear that even with the little roof we had, it wasn't very waterproof. Although the air was hot, I shivered as the warm rain soaked through my clothes, chilling me to the bone. It was if the thermostat had dropped thirty degrees in the room.

Eventually the rain died off and I struggled to get back to sleep. Even with the recent rain shower, the air was unforgiving as it sucked the moisture out of the air. I rolled over to one side but found it much hotter than the position I was just in. Finally I gave up and went outside to sit in front of the hut. I was just dozing off when I heard footsteps behind me. My head snapped up, all my senses on high alert.

"Chill out it just me," Bethany's voice floated from the hut. She was clutching a roll of toilet paper and was practically stumbling out of the hut.

"Bethany are you okay?" I asked. Her face looked look a tiny bit green.

"What? I'm fine. I have to go to the bathroom," she said and started headed for the woods.

"The bathroom's that way and you look a little sick," I pointed towards the outhouse.

"Nick said it wasn't finished yet, remember?" She smirked, "My face is green because I saved some of my face mask. It does wonders for the pores. Maybe you should try it?" She smirked again and with a flip of her hair, was off to the woods. I wasn't aware I was reaching to touch my face until my fingertips grazed my cheek. I shouldn't have let her torment me until I had insecurities. Suddenly, a high shrill shriek came from the woods and my mind shifted into gear. What animals were on the island? Don't know. Poisonous animals? Don't know. Man, why didn't we know this stuff. Before I could even get up to react to Bethany's scream, a twig snapped to my right, sending my hairs on my neck straight into the air. Slowly, I turned around and saw a black shape slink out of the forest in front of me. I couldn't move. Standing before me, crouched and ready to pounce, was a black jaguar baring its fangs. That's when I had to let out my own scream. I remembered when we went on that nature hike at the island we visited, they talked about jaguars. Who knew that I would actually see one.

The jaguar was slowly starting to circle and was a few feet away from me. The jaguar repositioned himself, and just before I saw my life flash before my eyes, Nick and Colby were there, throwing rocks at the jaguar and shouting. I shakily stood to my feet just as the jaguar leaped back into the woods. I turned to my head just in time to see Caroline and Calvin racing to Bethany's rescue.

"You-you saved my life," I stammered, pointing at Nick and Colby.

"No big deal," Nick said at the same time Colby said, "You're welcome." Still shaken up at my near death experience, I headed back into the now slightly cooler hut and settled in for a good night's sleep. I easily could have been devoured by that jaguar. It irked me a bit that it was Nick and Colby that saved my life. I'm not one for the whole damsel in distress thing. Closing my eyes, I was ready to drift off to sleep. That was before I heard the shouting.

"I can't believe you screamed bloody murder for something so little!" Caroline yelled, probably at Bethany. Groggily, I once again stepped out of the hut and found Caroline and Bethany, eyes wild, circling each other like hungry lions trying to protect their young.

"What's going on?" I questioned Emilia who was staring at the encounter as if it was a juicy cheeseburger and she hadn't eaten in weeks.

"When you were getting sized up by a jaguar, we thought Bethany was in danger too. Turns out, her bloody scream was because a bug landed on her," She whispered, still watching Caroline and Bethany intently.

"It's not my fault a bug landed on me! It was gross and slimy!" Bethany shrieked, putting her hands on her hips.

"So what! Monica here was about to get eaten by a jaguar and we thought you were too!" Caroline screamed back.

"I was getting attacked by a bug!" Bethany's face was growing red with rage.

"You're such a princess! All you care about is yourself! Oh look I'm Bethany! Isn't my hair *gorgeous*? I think I'll flip it fifty times!" Caroline over exaggerated her interpretation of Bethany by swinging her hips and flicking her hair. I hadn't know Caroline for long, but I could tell that this was totally out of character for her. Bethany took a threatening step towards her.

"Listen bitch," She started.

"Caroline back off," Calvin put his hands on Caroline's shoulders, preventing her from turning this into a real fight.

"No! Don't you get it? She thinks everyone should just care about her all the time and I'm sick of it! Rescue hasn't come and maybe it never will! But I am sick of *her*," Caroline was still worked up. That's when Bethany lunged. Colby stepped in and wrapped his arms around Bethany's middle and lifted her away from Caroline.

"Bethany calm down," Colby told her in a melt your heart kind of way. He wasn't even speaking to me and I got chills. Slowly, Caroline's face turned back to its normal complexion and she stomped inside. Calvin followed at her heels. Bethany did the same, although she stormed off towards the waterfall with Colby.

"Well that was certainly interesting," Bidziil said while yawning. His yawn was contagious and I suddenly remembered how tired I was.

"Whoa," Nick said as he caught me from falling. I blinked at him, not really sure what just happened but all I knew was that I was in his arms. I felt him guide me back to the hut and lay me down to sleep. No sooner than he lay down next to me, that I completely zonked out.

"Woohoo! We have our own hut!" Caroline punched the humid air with her fist shortly after we finished building the last hut which was the boy's.

"Hey y'all I think we should cool off," Calvin suggested and wiggled his eyebrows. He tore his sweaty shirt off in the island sun and picked up Caroline by the waist.

"Calvin!" she shrieked, half laughing, "Put me down!" Calvin laughed and but didn't listen to her and carried Caroline over to the pool. He threw her over his broad freckled shoulder and tossed her like a doll into the pool.

"Calvin!" She screamed when she screamed when she resurfaced. Her face was bright red, but it wasn't from the heat. "I can't believe you did that! Now my clothes are all wet!" Caroline splashed him.

"What? You looked like you were hot," he winked at her. Groans came from the guys and Emilia giggled. Bethany was already inside the girl's hut, not even bothering to help with the rest of the building after that was finished. I headed over towards the living room hut. We now called it the Canopy because of the opening roof Bidziil managed to create. I needed to cool off and the Canopy had the most shade. Plus, I had just jumped in the pool half an hour ago and my clothes were still a little damp.

"You're not coming for a swim?" Nick asked, coming to stand in the doorway. I smiled lightly but really, I just needed my privacy right now.

"No, I don't want to get my hair wet again and I kind of want to be alone," I blushed. I needed to change my damp clothes without Bethany being in the room smirking at me. When Nick turned to go, I caught a glimpse of a sigh drooping off his shoulders. Before I could think anything of it, I turned my back on the doorway and resumed changing my clothes. Fortunately, it was my day to wear the extra shirt.

The warm air blew through the half wall. Why was it that on a chilly night, the breeze was still warm? It made no sense. Sighing, I headed to the girl's hut, hearing distant laughter. We had recently strung together surprisingly strong hammocks out of the vines. As I entered the hut, Caroline's voice drifted to my ears.

"I've known him for what, two weeks? I can't tell if I like him," she said. She was soaking wet sitting on her hammock, which was unfortunately above mine.

"Like who?" I asked, coming into view.

"I think Calvin likes Caroline but Caroline doesn't know if she likes him," Emilia explained. She was lying on the hammock above Bethany who appeared to be asleep with her arm across her eyes.

"How do I know I like him if we've known each other for only two weeks? I mean look at Colby. He likes you, but do you know if you like him? You couldn't. It's been *two weeks*," Caroline sounded like a teenage therapist. I snorted.

"I do *not* like Colby," I stated. Although I tried to be serious, I felt a blush making its way across my face.

"Please, you so do, you can see it in your eyes when he looks at you," Caroline argued as I settled into my hammock. I brushed away a droplet of water coming from Caroline only to have it be replaced not even two seconds later.

"She doesn't like Colby, she likes Nick," Emily announced.

"What?!" I quickly sat up, banging my head on Caroline's leg.

"Ow!" We yelled at the same time. Bubbles of laughter began coming from Caroline uncontrollably.

"You so do," Caroline said in between breaths.

"Do not!"

"Do too!"

"Do not!"

"Do too!"

"Do not!"

"Do too!" Nick's voice came from the guy's hut which was on the other side of the Canopy.

"Nick! I yelled at him. Peals of laughter came from their hut. I glanced nervously at Caroline. How much did they hear? Crunching on the dirt came from the doorway and we all turned to see Nick standing there.

"What did you hear?" I demanded.

"Not much, just you and Caroline screaming over and over. It was Colby's idea for me to shout that," Nick shrugged. He and the other guys had no idea what we were talking about.

"Good," I nodded. Nick smiled lightly and I felt my heart begin to flutter. I was still standing there a couple seconds after he left.

"Oh my gosh you do like him!" Emilia squealed from her bunk. I just rolled my eyes, not wanting to get into the argument again. Climbing onto my bunk, I tried drifting off to sleep. After about an hour, with soft sounds of sleep coming from all directions, I sat up and stepped outside. I sat down on the ground outside of the hut and looked up at the stars. I tried to pick out any constellations but unfortunately all the ones I knew were back at home with everything else I knew. I sat like that for a while, just staring at the stars. I could hear the snores coming from the boy's hut along with a quiet muttering. Someone must have been talking in their sleep.

My thoughts drifted and soon I found myself thinking of the night I almost became cat food. Just thinking about it made the back of my neck stand up and suddenly I was aware of every sound. The jungle made weird noises at night and when you're by yourself, it seemed as though an axe murder was going to pop out from behind a tree at anytime. Creepy thoughts aside, I bolted into the hut and attempted to go back to sleep. It wasn't that easy. I awoke only about an hour later to the sound of hard rain on the hut's roof. What was with the island and its frequent rain storms? A couple of rain droplets leaked through the roof and splashed my arm. I groaned and rolled over. I just wanted to go home.

That thought crossed my mind but then I realized, did I really want to go *home* or did I just want to get off the island? Home wasn't so ideal. It seemed as though it was temporary. A place that I was just visiting but never really living in. If I was just visiting the place that I grew up in and was raised in, then where was my true home? Was it on the dreadful island? Was it in a big city or a small town? Was it in a different country or on the West or East coast? How would I even know? Would I just feel like I belonged? But that was a scary thought. What if I never found a place where I belonged?

CHAPTER 7: 1 WEEK AND 1 DAY AFTER SHIPWRECK

"We should try to find a way off this island," Nick announced at breakfast the next morning. I took a swig of coconut milk and let him continue. After last night, I felt ready for anything. Nick mimicked me and took a drink out of his coconut. Some milk dribbled down his chin and I fought a strange urge to wipe it away. Funny. I had always gone for lighter haired guys. Guys like Colby.

"What do y'all have in mind?" Calvin asked, leaning back on his elbows.

"Well," Nick started, "we could look around the jungle first to see.."

"Nuh uh! I am *not* going in *there*!" Bethany interrupted. Nick glared at her.

"You wouldn't have to go. Anyway, if we look in the forest, maybe there is a civilization or something not too far from here. We should do that before anything drastic," Nick concluded. Caroline and I nodded in unison and then laughed.

"Sounds like a plan," Emilia agreed, already wiping sweat off her forehead. Her long black uniform skirt was making her cook like a baked potato.

"Emilia you're overheating. You can't wear that forever," I stood up and brushed dirt off my shorts. Emilia looked at me suspiciously.

"I'm fine," she said stubbornly. We all gave her a look.

"Emilia we're serious. If you don't do something about it, it could be fatal," Bidziil recited. Emilia gulped and slowly stood. We headed into the girl's hut and I knelt by the hem of her skirt and tugged at the material. Shudders from her knees created ripples in the fabric. Finally, I small rip formed and I used that to tear off a layer of the skirt. Emilia whimpered at the sound of the fabric being destroyed. I gave the skirt one final tug, making it permanently knee length instead of ankle length.

"This is a disgrace to my school!" Emilia screeched when she looked down and saw what I had done. I straightened myself and looked her in the eye.

"Would you rather disgrace your school, which can't even see you, or die of heat stroke?" I asked and was about to head out into the sunlight when sobbing filled the air. I sighed.

"Emilia, you shouldn't worry about your school. Right now, you need to worry about yourself," I said gently, afraid of upsetting her even more. Instead, she shook her head and wrapped me in the biggest hug I ever had.

"Thank you. I've been wanting to rip that skirt for the longest time. I'm sick of wearing them," she laughed into my shoulder and soon we were both on the floor collapsing in laughter.

As we approached our little group, something dawned on me. Bidziil was staring open mouthed and bug eyed behind me. Slowly I smiled. Bidzill and Emilia. That seems completely perfect.

"Emilia, you look, you look, um, much cooler," Bidziil stuttered. Caroline and I shared a grin as I joined everyone on the ground.

"Yeah I am, but I have no idea what my mother would say if she saw me like this. I'd probably be grounded until I was thirty," Emilia laughed, a pink tint gracing her cheeks.

"Your mother would say 'I'm so glad you're alive, we thought you were dead'," Nick mumbled. I turned my head. Mother. Dead. Not the two words I like to use in a sentence. Coughing, I tried to change the subject.

"Are we heading into the jungle today or not?" I asked, looking pointedly at Nick.

My backpack weighed heavily on my shoulders as we trudged through the muddy terrain.

"Why do we have to carry these leaf things? Ew! My shoe!" Bethany squawked. She almost sounded like one of the annoying mosquitoes surrounding us. I didn't know they could come out during the day.

"We have to carry these backpacks so we can carry fresh water," Nick explained from ahead of me. An hour ago we created backpacks out of large palm leaves tied with small strips of vine. They all held small canisters of water pretty well. Caroline and I were keeping pace together while Emilia and Bidziil were talking quietly behind us. Bethany brought up the rear, making us look like a lost train with Nick, Colby and Calvin as the conductors. I pushed past another thick ivy covered branch and avoided a mud patch. The jungle kept getting denser and denser and we hadn't seen anything remotely close to human life. A parrot or two, but that was it.

"Nick, we've been pushing our way through the jungle for four hours, can we please take a break?" I begged. My feet were tired, I was panting, and I desperately needed a drink. Suddenly, the jungle became less dense and we emerged in front of a water pool. Our pool.

"You took us in a huge circle!" Calvin exclaimed, his face red with the head and slightly peeling.

"I didn't, I mean..." Nick tried to defend himself. It was if a ticking time bomb finally went off as everyone started fighting and yelling. Bethany lunged at Caroline and began pulling her hair. Colby, Calvin and Bidziil ganged up on Nick and started shoving. Baffled, I stood there for a couple minutes, then did the one thing I was told to do in a situation like this. I stuck two fingers in my mouth and blew, letting out a sharp whistle. Instantly everyone froze.

"Listen. We haven't seen any rescue ships or planes. We'll try to get off this island, but in the meantime, we'll have to get along. We can't be fighting. We've only known each other for a week and five days. I know, I've been counting. Why do we have to fight already? We're not some gang members who need to fight to the death. So Nick got us in a circle. So what? At least we're not lost in the jungle! Give him some credit," I concluded my speech. Thankfully, everyone cleared off towards the pool. Nick shot me a grateful look. I mouthed you're welcome. His mouth twitched then he winced and covered his left cheek with his hand.

"Did you get punched?" I gasped and stepped closer, moving his hand off of his face. It was rough, beginning to get calloused from the work we've done.

"Calvin got in a pretty good swing," he laughed halfheartedly.

"I wish we had some ice or something to put on it," I glanced at his wound. There was already a bruise forming under his eye.

"That's okay. I can deal with it," Nick shook his head but even that simple gesture made him wince in pain again.

"We have to find something. Maybe the first aid bag has something," I took Nick's hand and pulled him towards the Canopy. Crouching next to the bag, I dug deep and came up with a small ice pack. Unfortunately, it was the kind that you could heat up or chill by putting it in the microwave or freezer.

"We can soak that in the pool. It might help with the swelling," Nick suggested, his voice suddenly very close to my ear. I nodded.

"That's a good idea." We headed towards the pool where I dipped the pack into the water and let it absorb.

"Why don't we leave it here to soak, the water's shallow enough that we can just reach in and grab it," Nick pulled me to my feet and tugged me towards the diving rock.

"Do you think we'll get off this island?" I asked, not meeting his gaze. He said he had an idea.

"If my plan works, then yes, I think we will. It may take some time to build though," he said as we reached the top. We both stripped into our bathing suites and stood on the edge.

"Thanks for saving me back there," he said, locking his gaze on mine. My mouth instantly didn't know what o say and my body froze. It was that stare again. Nick's arm came towards me and brushed a lock of my hair away from my face. Just as he was leaning in, he jumped off the side into a cannon ball, yelling on the way down. I gave a shaky laugh. Part of my was relieved and part of me was extremely disappointed. Well, if we didn't start working on that plan he had cooking up soon, who knows how long it's going to take to get out of here. Instead of going down to camp and putting my mind to use, I let it go blank and dove.

Part 2: Survival

I sat and stared out at the royal blue horizon, desperately wishing to see an outline of a boat. Instead, the only shape I saw was the shadow of someone behind me.

"Hey Monica," Colby said in his soft voice. My heart started pounding instantly.

"Hi Colby," I said, keeping my voice steady. Colby sat on the sand next to me, our knees slightly touching.

"I've been meaning to ask you for a while now," Colby started. His voice sounded far away from all the pounding in my ears.

"Ask me what?" I asked, urging him on.

"Do you maybe want to come out here tonight to look at the stars?" He questioned while staring at the sea. The pounding in my heart stopped for a brief moment and then started up again. He was asking me out on a date! A date! Me! Romance wasn't on my agenda this summer, but then again neither was being a castaway.

"Okay. When should we meet? The only person who has a watch with them is Nick," I asked. For some reason, I didn't want Nick to know what we were going to do. Why was it that whenever I was with Nick, I thought about Colby, but when I was with Colby, I thought about Nick?

"Why don't we meet here when everyone's asleep," he said suggestively. A blush crept to my face but I nodded. Where we were sitting now was the only spot on the whole stretch of beach that wasn't covered when the tide came in.

"Great, I'll see you then," Colby slowly got up and walked out of sight. That's when I noticed I was grinning like an idiot and my hands were shaking. Dirt was caked under my fingernails and even though I took a dip in the pool every day, I still felt a layer of dirt permanently settled on my body. I would definitely have to clean up before my date with Colby. Date! I turned my eyes back to the ocean and began daydreaming. We've been here a month now and haven't seen nor heard a ship or plane. Often, it makes me wonder if they're looking for us at all. If the cruise had gone according to plan, I would have been at home with my friends, eating burgers and fries at the local diner right then; my secret weakness. Kayce and Rachel, my two best friends would be sharing gossip around the table about who was dating who. If the cruise had gone according to plan, I could have been lounging by the community pool instead of marooned on some island. If the cruise had gone according to plan, I would have had to see Emily Cox and Riley snuggling up at lunch every day when school started back up. I smiled, knowing the one and only good thing coming out of the island was preventing me from seeing *them* in two months. We probably weren't going to be rescued by then. The only other good thing that came out of the island was meeting Colby, Nick, Caroline, Emilia, Bidziil and Calvin. I purposely left out Bethany. I know I made some lifelong friends because we were probably going to be on the island for the rest of our lives. Was I ever going to finish High School, go to college, start a family? No, probably not, all because of the one cruise. And my dad. If he didn't force me to go in the first place, I could have been sitting at home watching T.V. at that moment. Wouldn't that be a treat? I was craving music, pizza, ice cream. I craved a nice warm bed and air conditioning. On the island it felt like we were transported into the past before any of that was invented. I almost expected to see a dinosaur pop up.

Slowly, I watched the sun set in a rainbow of colors. My stomach grumbled, warning me that I needed food or I would pass out. Heading back to camp, the smell of cooked fish slithered its way into my nose. Yay. Fish again. We've seen some little wild pigs around but none of us had the heart to kill them. I guess we were stuck with fish until we toughened up. Apparently, the fish were done cooking for a while because when I got there, there was only one left.

"I guess this is mine then," I mumbled to no one in particular.

"Calvin wanted that fish all to himself, but I saved it for you," Colby said as I sat on the sand. He winked.

"So where were you all this afternoon? It was like you disappeared," Caroline asked around a piece of fish.

"I was at the beach just looking at the water," I said like it was no big deal.

"Looking for ships or daydreaming?" Caroline smiled. I shrugged.

"A little bit of both."

"I'm a little nervous that this contraption isn't going to work," Caroline whispered, referring to Nick's plan to get us off the island.

"Me too. It would be awful if it backfired," I commented. Caroline nodded then yawned.

"I think I need to go to bed," she said and tossed her leaf plate into the fire. It made a crackling sound as she walked into the hut. My hands started shaking again with nerves. It was so much closer to the date! The last date I had had ended badly. I hope this one won't.

It was only two weeks after Riley broke up with me when Kayce and Rachel tried to get my butt off the couch and back into the game. Hey, I still needed to grieve. But I ended up going, and it was fine. Until the guy started crying. He broke down in the middle of bowling just crying like a baby. He was going on and on about how I looked like his ex-girlfriend. Between sobs, he told me they went out for two years and then he walked in on her making out with another guy. Apparently, it was going on for a year. I felt bad for the guy, but then I started crying about Riley and it was just not good.

So needless to say, my heart was hoping that the date didn't end in disaster as I walked towards the beach. Colby was already there, sitting on the dry patch of beach, his toes dipped in the shallow water at his feet.

"Hey," I said and sat down next to him.

"Wow, look up. There are so many stars," he was in awe. When I gazed up, I was in awe too. Millions and millions of stars scattered the sky like white paint on an artist's black canvas. It took my breath away.

"This is amazing," I breathed, lying back against the sand.

"I see stars like this back home, but not this many," he said and leaned back to where I was. Our arms slightly touched, sending silent tremors up and down my arm.

"Since it is Colorado, you would assume," I said, "Back home you can see stars only on clear nights. It gets cloudy pretty often. At least there's no city smog," I said, unaware of what I was saying.

"Wait. I thought you lived in Massachusetts," Colby noticed, "Massachusetts has city smog. I've been there."

"I-I do, but where I live, it's kind of rural," I stumbled, quickly covering up my mistake. This seemed to satisfy Colby, who turned his head to look back at the stars.

"Man. Who knew we had to come out to the middle of nowhere to see stars?" He commented, slightly shaking his head. I shrugged.

"I guess you kind of have to."

"If I had to be in the middle of nowhere with somebody, I'm glad it's you," Colby reached for my hand, sending an electric shock up my arm. It was weird. Colby's shock was static electricity compared to Nick's lighting. Oh well. Did he ask me out? No. He did not. Turning my head to glance at him, I asked,

"Why me?" I was honestly curious.

"You really want me to answer that?" He asked, a confused expression on his face. I felt my heart deflate a little. The fairytale bubble seemed to burst. I couldn't be toyed with. My heart just couldn't take much more.

"Colby, did you only ask me out so you could hook up with me?" I asked just a little annoyed. It was heading in a bad direction. How could a hot guy like Colby like a normal girl like me? Maybe being on a deserted island makes you delusional.

"Of course not. There's much more to you than that," he said and squeezed my hand. Instantly I felt a bit better.

"Hey look a shooting star," Colby suddenly pointed to the sky. I glanced up just in time to see it streak by.

"Make a wish," Colby whispered. And I did. I wished we were off the island!

My hammock swung slowly in the warm breeze. Adrenaline from my date pulsed through my veins, preventing me from falling asleep.

"Monica are you still up?" Caroline called sleepily from above. I had no idea she was still awake.

"Yeah," I called back wearily.

"Where did you go for that long time?" She asked, rolling over on her stomach so I could see her face.

"Promise you won't tell anyone?" I questioned. I didn't want everyone to know. Not yet.

"I promise," Caroline yawned.

"Colby asked me to go look at the stars with him. It was kind of a date," I answered, flipping to my side.

"Really?!" She squealed, suddenly bolting upright.

"Shh! Caroline keep it down!" I hissed. Caroline threw her hand over her mouth and mumbled sorry.

"Was it fun?" She whispered.

"Yes, it was fun," I smiled and flipped to my stomach, officially closing the conversation. Caroline got my drift and I heard her shift above. Soon, the hut was completely silent and I could just barely hear the boys snoring. Between the rhythm of my hammock rocking and the snoring, I fell fast asleep.

"Oh my god! Monica wake up! You have to see this!," Caroline rocked my hammock, threatening to tip it over.

"What, what! I'm up! Just don't let me face plant on to the ground," I huffed and followed her out of the hut. Immediately, as I stepped into the air, something was different. The air had a sense of anticipation running currents through the cool breeze. Cool breeze. The island never had a cool breeze. Wind jostled the leaves of the palm that stood near the outhouse, bringing a new smell in its wake. The smell of a damp Earth.

Caroline was running towards the beach where the rest of our crew was staring in awe at the horizon. I pushed my way to the front to get a look.

"What's going on? Is it a ship?" I asked frantically. Nick, who was staring next to me said nothing and just pointed. Confused, I dragged my gaze towards where the ocean met the sky. Waves, at least ten feet high crashed together on the shore. Night dark clouds littered the sky, creating an ominous feeling in the air. Suddenly I understood the signs. We were in for it big time.

"How long do you think until the storm hits shore?" I asked under my breath to Nick. He shrugged.

"It could be seconds, minutes, hours," he said in a slow monotone.

"How bad of a storm do you think it's going to be?" Calvin asked from behind me.

"Well since it's summertime and we're in the tropics, I think it's going to hit tropical storm level," Bidziil concluded, sounding like a stuffy college professor.

"Where are we going to go?" Emilia asked shakily. Nick seemed to ponder this and then his eyes lit up. He sprinted back to the forest and puzzled, we followed him. Panting, we caught up to Speedy Gonzalez as he was scaling the rocks near the waterfall.

"Nick! You're going to fall into the water!" Caroline shouted. Nick just shook his head, getting drenched by the waterfall. As if in slow motion, he swung his legs and jumped through the waterfall. I cringed, waiting for a splash. It never came.

"Nick?" I called, heading towards the waterfall.

"In here!" I heard his voice eco. Then I saw his black hair and his dazzling blue eyes poke out from *behind* the waterfall.

"I discovered this a couple days ago and this would be the perfect place to wait out the storm. Here come on in!" he disappeared back into the cave. Scaling the waterfall wall by putting my feet in small ledges like a saw Nick do, I made my way to the opening. Ignoring the waterfall drenching my hair, I fell into the cave.

The cave was a lot bigger than I imagined it to be. It could easily hold all eight of us by continuing in the back where it got just a little bit hotter.

"This goes under the mountain doesn't it," I realized.

"Part of it. I went all the way to the back when I found it and it just ends," Nick shrugged. I heard the slap of sneakers hitting the cave floor and turned to see Caroline, Calvin, Bidziil, Emilia and Colby drop in. No surprise Bethany didn't come.

"This is perfect," was all we needed to say.

"It's nice and dry in here so it would protect us from the storm," Calvin studied in the cave, "Although the opening would be wet from the waterfall."

"We could just huddle in the back," Colby suggested, showing his hidden smart side.

"That just might work. Who knew Pretty Boy was smart?" Nick commented.

"I'm not all good looks, right Monica?" he slung his arm around my shoulders, making my heart constrict.

"Right," I managed. Nick stared at us as if we were a scary movie. Horrifying, yet you can't look away. Only after a few terrifying seconds, he tore away his gaze.

"Okay then. I guess we should start bringing supplies down here," Nick said softly and headed for the pool and jumped. This time I heard a splash. Smoothly, I plunged into the cool pool after him and surfaced for air near the edge. Nick was already out and grabbing our extra palm leaves.

"What are those for?" Bidziil asked as he climbed out beside me and shook dripping hair like a dog. Emilia giggled.

"I'm not sure yet. Maybe we'll just save them from blowing away in the wind," Nick said, holding up the leaves to examine. I rung out my hair and started gathering up the first aid bag.

"Try to get everything that we absolutely need so we can take it back to the cave," I instructed. I followed Caroline into our hut where she picked up all our blankets.

"Just in case it's cold," she explained, already heading towards the boy's hut to gather their blankets. I took a glance around the room and grabbed my bag that had washed ashore and stuffed in my picture, letter and the other girls few belongings that were lying around the room. We definitely didn't want to lose those. I headed back outside and saw everyone, except Bethany of course, frantically gathering up supplies while keeping an eye on the sky. Hesitantly, I lifted my head to the darkened clouds. It was then that I noticed the wind had picked up. The storm was closing in around our island fast. Sprinting now, I collected the rest of our supplies and followed the others to the cave.

Climbing successfully into the cave without getting wet, my feet carried me to the back of the cave where Bethany, Colby, Emilia and Caroline were huddled.

"Where are Nick, Calvin and Bidziil?" I asked placing my bag and other items I found on the floor of the cave.

"Probably outside keeping an eye on the storm," Emilia suggested while going through the items I had gathered.

"Okay," I wiped my hands on my shorts and headed towards the opening. Just then, Calvin and Bidziil dropped in, right in front of me.

"Ahh!" They screamed, not expecting me to be there. I bit back laughter and grasped the first rock that would pull me up to the ground above the waterfall. Nick was sitting near the stream that led to the waterfall. His head was lifted to the sky in a puzzled expression.

"Hey," I said coming to sit next to him. Static electricity buzzed in the air. Was it from the coming storm or that Nick and I were so close to each other?

"Hey," he said, not taking his eyes off the clouds.

"Are you worried about the storm?" I asked, not being able to read his expression.

"I don't know how we're going to survive this storm. If it really is a tropical storm, then we are in for some trouble," he answered, finally lowering his head to look me in the eyes. His blue eyes weren't at the brightest I've seen them. They looked almost hurt. I sighed.

"Nick, first off, your plan is going to work. Second, what's really wrong? I'm your friend, acquaintance, whatever. You can talk to me," I said gently, placing my hand onto his.

"I know I can talk to you because you've told me things before. But this, I can't tell you," he turned his head away from me. A nagging thought tugged at my brain.

"Last month, when we first got shipwrecked, you said that you didn't have a choice to come on the cruise. What did you mean?" I asked. He sighed.

"When I won the school contest, I didn't want to go on this trip. My friends and I only put our names in as a joke. My stepmom, Laura, told me I had to go on the trip so that while I was away, she and my dad could go to France. I bet they don't even care that we've been shipwrecked," Nick spoke softly, not wanting the others to hear. I understood that feeling.

"I have a confession. My school wasn't having a drawing for the trip. When my dad read about the cruise in the newspaper and how Cainbridge High in Massachusetts backed out, he told me to say that was where I was from. He only put me on the cruise so he could have the house all to himself and his lady "friends". I'm really from Wisconsin," I said softly too.

"Sounds like we have pretty messed up family lives and well *our* lives," he shrugged. I felt he first raindrop land on my shoulder.

"Yeah, I guess we do," I stood.

"But one good thing did come out of this," Nick smiled slightly.

"What?" I asked, a little suspicious.

"I met you," he answered and then disappeared over the waterfall. Stunned, I hung back. More drops began hitting my shoulders and I ran after him. The wind was picking up and with my hand on the rocks, I began the climb down.

"Calvin stop! You're getting me wet!" Caroline shrieked in my ear. She and Calvin were sitting close to the waterfall, him flicking droplets of water at her.

"It's really starting to storm out there. Maybe you should move away from the opening, I suggested, my feet gently landing on to the ground. A crack of thunder ripped through the sky. Emilia squeaked like she was part guinea pig and scampered to the back of the cave to hide behind Bidziil. Who was enjoying the attention, judging by the size of the grin on his face. Another crack of thunder sounded, sending Caroline and Calvin scurrying away from the cave opening. Normally, I don't mind thunderstorms. But considering that this was a *tropical* thunderstorm, I was freaked. Making my way to the back of the cave, the air grew denser and damper. I stuck my sweaty palms into my back pockets, clutching my photograph. The edges were worn from all the times I depended on it for comfort, but I didn't mind.

"I *hate* storms. They make my hair go frizzy," Bethany whined, edging herself closer to Colby. Colby's eyes were locked onto my from the moment I sat on the rocky ground. It was that stare again. Did every girl get harassed with stares like those? Not that I minded them from Colby. Or Nick. How could two guys both make me feel something, but the feeling was different at the same time?

"Anyone for blankets?" Caroline asked, holding up one of our blankets from the hammocks.

"I am, it actually got chilly," Nick said. Now that he mentioned it, a shiver rippled through my body and I reached out to get a blanket too.

"Island weather is so weird," Emilia commented, "When I lived in England, you could always expect the weather. It was always dreary except in the summer when it was sunny. We were lucky we lived near the beach on those sunny days. I used to take my sister down and play in the sand."

"I didn't know you had a sister," I said, wrapping the thinly weaved blanket we made around my body.

"Actually I have two. Veronica and Georgia. Veronica's twelve and Georgia's eight. I really do miss them. And mum," Emilia sniffled.

"What about your dad?" Calvin asked, leaning back against the cave wall.

"He's back in England. Mum and him got divorced when I was sixteen. That's when we moved to the U.S.," Emilia said with no emotion.

"But you don't miss him?" Caroline asked.

"No. He never did treat my mum quite right. I'm surprised she put up with it so long," Emilia turned away from us and faced the waterfall that was spraying the cave with water.

"That's how it was with my parents," I heard myself say. Where did that come from? We're all in an enclosed cave and suddenly we're telling each other our secrets?

"What do you mean?" Emilia asked, turning back to the group.

"My dad is a liar, a cheat and an abuser. One day she had enough. I was fifteen and she told me we were going to my

Grandma's. We never made it. She was going too fast and crashed head first into another car. She died on impact," I said softly.

"God. That must have been awful," Bidziil whispered. I nodded; I couldn't show my face to them. Tears were streaming down it. Slowly, I glanced at Caroline who just looked at me with her mouth wide open. Something warm clasped my hand and I turned to see Nick's hand covering mine.

"At least *my* family's perfect," Bethany boasted with her signature toss of her hair.

"Nobody's family is," I said quietly, making sure that I could only hear myself. Nick squeezed my hand.

The wind howled outside, making the cave have an eerie effect. Without realizing it, I huddled closer to Nick. Somewhere outside a seagull called. You would think that they would have already taken cover.

"Who wants to play a game?" I asked, trying to lighten the mood.

"What did you have in mind?" asked Caroline, picking up on my topic change.

"How about two truths and a lie? It was a game that I played when I was in middle school," I suggested.

"What's that?" Colby tilted his head.

"You think of two truths about yourself or things that you did and one lie. Everyone else has to guess the lie," I explained just as another roll of thunder hit the sky.

"Sounds fun. Who wants to go first?" Nick nodded.

"I'll go," Bethany suggested, staring at her nails, "I've been scuba diving twice, I have a boyfriend back home named Mark and I was head cheerleader at my school even though I was only a junior." Our little group pretended to ponder over this but we already knew the lie.

"Is it you have a boyfriend named Mark?" Colby asked, turning to face her.

"Yup, I'm totally single," she flirted. Unfortunately, Colby was buying her act.

"Colby should go now that he got the lie," I suggested, pulling them out of a lovey dovey situation.

"Okay um, I brought the football team to the state championships three times, I have a dog named Scout and when I was little, my sisters used to paint my toenails red," he said while playing with his shoelaces. I laughed. Red? Seriously?

"Ok, ok I got this. It's that your sisters used to paint your toenails red," Bidziil said laughing.

"Nope," Colby blushed a cute pink. That just made us laugh even harder.

"Seriously dude?" Calvin asked, practically on the ground he was laughing so hard.

"Guess again," was all Colby said.

"Is it that you brought the football team to the state championships three times?" Nick asked.

"Yeah. I never brought them to the championships. I wish I had though," Colby nodded.

"Aw, well you'll get them next time. That would be a big accomplishment," Bethany cooed. She was obviously trying to piss someone off. Was that her actual flirting style? Jeez, would she like some nachos with that cheese? Glancing up form my gaze at the ground, a sinking feeling about the size of my heard dropped to my stomach. It was a feeling which I thought was only possible in romance novels. Colby was *actually* buying her act.

"Well, you know being head cheerleader at your school is a pretty big accomplishment too," Colby flirted back. What?! How come he was flirting with her when I'm the one he asked out? Am I not the only one he asked out? Dread filled my sunken heart and I tried my best to put a mask on to hide my pain. Locking gazes with Caroline, I rolled my eyes to show how corny the situation was. She responded with a classic gay motion: finger pointing down throat. I snorted.

"What's so funny?" Nick whispered in my ear. Shivers of who knows what floated down my bloodstream form my ear to my toes and then to my brain, clogging it.

"N-nothing," I stuttered. Got that's embarrassing. How was it that I felt such passion for both boys? I look one way and I was upset over Colby, I look another way and I'm falling over Nick! My hand slid from my knee, where I was hugging them to my chest, and hit the ground. As if on cue, the second my pinky lightly touched his pinky, the cave lit up and thunder rolled above us. How cliché. Energy flowed through us, making my hair at the base of my neck stand on end. I glanced cautiously at Nick. Had he felt it too? He wasn't even looking in my direction.

"I think we should continue our game," I said to break the now awkward silence, "I'll go next. I had a dog named Mickey

Mouse when I was little, I accidentally killed two goldfish by dropping my cell phone charger in the fish tank, and I used to have cucumber and cream cheese sandwiches everyday at lunch in fourth grade."

"I think I know what it is," Emilia's hand shot in the air, waving fiercely.

"Emilia, you don't really need to raise your hand," I corrected and giggled at her proper ways.

"Oh, right. Sorry. I think the like is that you ate cucumber and cream cheese sandwiches everyday at lunch?" she guessed incorrectly.

"Nope," I smirked.

"Is it that you *accidentally* killed your goldfish?" questioned Caroline.

"Nope."

"Well that it has to be that you had a dog named Mickey Mouse," said Nick in a slightly adorable know it all way.

"That's the lie. I never had a dog. We couldn't afford one," I explained. An especially loud clap of thunder shook the cave, making me jump, hitting my arm against Nick's leg. Another one of those sparks of electricity bounced off his arm and onto mine. It was like getting a shot from the energizer bunny. Apparently, Nick didn't feel this one either.

"Do you think we're going to have enough to eat?" Bidziil asked, eyeing our pile of fruits.

"I think so. The most we're probably going to be stuck in here is about two or three days. It depends," Nick said, eyeing the fruit as well. My stomach rumbled the second I turned to see the fruit for myself.

"Hungry? Here have a mango," Nick tossed a plump mango in my direction.

"Thanks," I squeaked and bit into the tender fruit. The tickle of juice dribbled down my chin but I didn't bother to wipe it away, knowing that in about a second, I wouldn't need to wipe away another one. Biting into the fruit again, it reminded me of when my mother and I would go peach picking in the summer.

My mother would bring me to an orchard one of her friends from college owned. I remember going up and down the rows of peach trees, looking for the perfect peach. One summer, I found it. The peach was round and a perfect shade of pinkish yellow.

"That's the one mommy," I said in my little kid voice. I was only eight at the time.

"That one? Are you sure?" She always asked this question. I had a habit of finding a better peach the moment she picked it.

"Yes," I said and put my scrawny arms on my hips. My mom reached high into the tree and pulled out my perfect peach. As I bit into it, the taste was sour and uncomfortable in my mouth. It was at that moment that I realized, not everything in life is perfect. It may seem that way on the outside, but inside was another story.

Thinking of my mother and the peach orchard made me think of home. I had given up all possible hope of rescue. Safety wasn't registered in my brain anymore. We couldn't rely on being rescued. If we wanted to get off the island, we would have to rescue ourselves. Nick's plan was simple. If it worked, then we would be out of there. If it didn't…I didn't want to think what would happen.

Walking to the cave's entrance, I risked a peak outside. The sky looked threatening as thick clouds meandered through the air. A streak of lightning lit up the sky, outlining the ominous clouds in a golden hue. Palm trees were bending in the harsh wind and the waterfall was splashing my face. As another crack of thunder rolled through the storm, I crept back to the group. Calvin was sleep with his head tilted back and snoring. Everyone was subdued, just listening to the rain outside. One by one, everyone slowly fell asleep. Everyone except for me and Colby that is.

"So," he whispered, careful not to wake anyone.

"So," I mimicked.

"So, you like me right?" Colby asked bluntly. I guess he didn't like keeping secrets. His question made me blush.

"Well…I guess…I mean," I stuttered. I focused my gaze on the opposite wall. I couldn't look him in his hypnotizing eyes.

"I'll take that as a yes," he slid next to me and put his arm around my shoulders. I expected it to feel nice there, like his arm belonged on my shoulders. But it felt out of place. I looked over at Nick who was sleeping peacefully beside me. For some reason, I felt guilty. Strands of his black hair lightly grazed his forehead. Oddly enough, I wanted to brush them away.

"Colby, I think this is moving too fast," I blurted out. Shock took a hold of Colby's face.

"Why?" he asked, "Isn't this what you want?"

"Well...I mean...yes but I don't know," I sighed. A sloppy grin formed on his tempting lips.

"Let me make up your mind," he whispered and then dipped his head to kiss me. I should have backed away or done something, but I didn't. I guess I just wanted to see if sparks would fly. Having his lips pressed against mine, well, I was melting. But only slightly. I was aware of Nick's shifting position on the floor. Colby pulled away from me and I grinned up at him. Slowly I got up and listened for anymore thunder. Not hearing anything, I moved closer to the waterfall and dove into the pool. Warm water enclosed around me, muffling any sound. The current wasn't too rough and I stayed underwater as long as I could to clear my head. Finally surfacing, I squinted against the downpour of rain. It was beginning to thin out and a hint of the moon shone out from the clouds. Flipping over, I looked towards our huts. Or what used to be them.

"Oh my god!" I screamed and splashed ashore, running to the ruins of our shelter. Hearing my cries, Calvin and Caroline climbed out of the cave. Branches, vines and anything else you could imagine, was lying on top of the huts, flattening them like pancakes. The wind was dying the down indicating that the storm was almost over.

"Monica come back into the cave, we can't do anything about it now," Calvin held out his hand to pull me up from the sitting position I now was in. I took his hand, following him and Caroline back to the cave. I loathed going back to the cave, being so close to Colby. I seriously couldn't sort out my feelings. I was attracted to him but god, what had I gotten myself into? Entering the cave, I saw that Bidziil, Emilia and Bethany were still asleep while Colby and Nick stared awkwardly at anywhere but each other. Calvin and Caroline settled in, Caroline's head resting on Calvin's shoulder, and immediately drifted off to sleep. It was just me and two boys that I was incredibly attracted too. Great. Nick turned his head away from me and Colby just played with his laces. Each of them had open spots next to them. They practically begged me to make a choice. Surprising myself, I chose the one next to Nick. He hardly even noticed. Colby on the other hand began pretending to go to sleep. I waited until I could hear everyone's quiet breathing before I spoke.

"Are you mad at me?" It was the only reason I could think of.

"No," he replied, still not looking at me.

"Then why won't you look at me?" I asked him. He was being ridiculous. He turned and coldly stared at me. No emotion. Hollow. For some reason, it gave me chills. He turned back around.

"Happy now?"

"Very," I replied sarcastically, begging my voice not to quiver. It did anyway. Nick sighed.

"Look, I'm not mad, or anything, it's nothing I can explain," he said, not exactly facing me, but close.

"Okay, but just so you know, I'm still your friend, or acquaintance, you don't have to keep secrets from me," I told him, facing the other way. Chilly air passed through the cave, and unfortunately for me, Calvin was sitting on my blanket. I visibly shook and tried to warm my legs by tucking them into my chest.

"You cold?" Nick asked as he pulled on his blanket. I nodded.

"Come here," he opened up his blanket and motioned me to get under it. With him.

"Thanks," my teeth chattered as more air came in from the opening. I got under the small blanket, instantly feeling warmer.

"No problem," he put his arm around me as I continued to shiver. His arm felt like it belonged around me shoulders. As if it was perfectly sculpted to fit them. Nick's body heat radiated on me, and I was aware at just how close we were. Not yet touching, I made sure of that.

"You're my friend Monica. You could never be just an acquaintance," Nick didn't speak directly to me and he rested his head against the cave wall. Pretty soon, Nick dosed off and it was just me. With the wind still howling, quieter now, and the rain a soft pattern, I drifted off to sleep.

When I awoke, I could tell it was early. I felt something solid under my head and at first I thought it was the ground. Then I realized the ground didn't breathe. I slowly lifted my head off Nick's chest where it had positioned itself sometime during the night, and stretched out the kinks in my back. Ears straining, I listened for the wind. Nothing.

"Nick! Nick wake up!" I nudged him. He snorted and I couldn't help but laugh softly.

"Huh? What?" he lifted his head and looked at me sleepily. I slow smile spread across his lips.

"Listen," I whispered, not wanting to wake the others yet. I liked it just being Nick and me.

"I don't hear anything," he glanced at me, puzzled.

"Exactly," I mimicked his smiled. Recognition lit up his handsome face and he pulled me to my feet.

"Come on," he held onto my hand as we climbed out of the cave.

"Monica look," he pointed towards the sky once we were on flat land. I tilted my head and looked up. The sky was a perfect robin's eggs blue with absolutely no clouds in the sky.

"It's over," he sighed. I noticed he was still holding my hand. Did he feel the electric current that was running through my hand too? My gaze drifted over the to where our huts were.

"Nick!" I raised a shaky hand and pointed to the massive pile of vines and sticks that now inhabited where our huts used to be.

"Is that..." he stopped. I nodded and started over to the pile, flabbergasted.

"We'll have to rebuild. We can't live in the cave forever," Nick said coming up to my side.

"What do you mean forever? We're going home right?" Someone asked from behind us. Startled, I jumped about two feet in the air. Bethany was standing behind Nick with her hands on her hips, and flicking her hair. Again.

"it was just a figure of speech. I don't think we'll be here forever. Not if my plan works," Nick's eyes widened. "My plan!" He raced to the beach where we had secured our newly crafted bamboo raft to the trees. As I entered the beach, Nick was kneeling on the damp sand, inspecting the raft for damage.

"Amazing," he whispered to himself, "It held together during the storm." His voice was in awe.

"Wow. Do you think we could try it today?" I asked, helping him untie the vines we tied it to.

"Maybe. I guess it would make sense. That way we won't have to rebuild our huts," Nick nodded, pondering this.

"The only problem is deciding who should go," I noted. By now, the rest of us were gathered on the beach, gaping over the damage the storm did. I stared at he aqua water lapping at the shore. A hermit crab crawled lazily along. The crab had it good, I wouldn't mind being him. Or her? They don't have to worry about rebuilding their home, they carry it on their backs. But when they grow out of their home, they can just find a new one. A squawk sounded above and the next think I know, that hermit crab was being carried off by a seagull. Never mind.

"Aren't you going to help?" Nick's soft voice drew me out of my daydream.

"Oh, yeah sure," I stupidly said, internally smacking myself. My calloused fingers grabbed a hold of the raft and together, Nick, Bidziil and I heaved it upright, leaning it against a tree.

"Can I say now that I really don't want to go on the raft?" Emilia raised her hand, once again forgetting that we weren't in school. And probably never will be again.

"You don't have to go on the raft," Calvin said, scratching at his leg where a mosquito had bitten him.

"Right. I vote that Monica and Colby go," Caroline said, winking. She didn't know how much I didn't like that kiss. Or that he even kissed me at all.

"I'll go. Monica you up for a challenge?" Colby raised his blonde eyebrows at me, and despite my poking feeling of confusion, I had to smile.

"Fine. Let's go," I tried to hide my nervousness of being out on the water. Something wasn't quite right about the raft idea, even though I kept telling Nick that his plan was going to work. It would work if we go according to schedule, reach an island, get help and *not* have our raft sink. Timidly, I placed the raft on top of the water and turned to my friends as Colby held the raft. Caroline came up and hugged me.

"Have fun with Colby," she giggled into my ear. I just nodded. Now wasn't the time to get into detail. Nick stepped forward, surprising me with a hug. Just like Caroline he whispered something in my ear.

"Get us home."

Colby cleared his throat and I pulled away from Nick hoping that the next time I saw him, it would be on a rescue boat heading away from the island. Colby and I pushed the raft out into deeper water and then climbed on, the bamboo wobbling slightly. Soon, we were afloat, using our makeshift paddles to steer in the direction that Nick said we should go in. The island grew tinier and tinier, until I couldn't see it anymore. Panic washed over me. We didn't have any food or water. What if we were going in the wrong direction? What if we ended up on another deserted island? What if we got surrounded by sharks again? What if-

"Monica, you okay?" Colby asked, staring at me quizzically.

"What? Yeah I'm fine. Just thinking," I faced my gaze to the horizon, searching for an outline of an island or boat.

"About me I hope," Colby smirked. I winced. Cheesy.

"Actually no, I wasn't," I said absent mindedly. My arms were getting tired, and I noticed a change in the wind.

"Colby are you sure we're headed in the right direction?" I asked unsure of the dark approaching clouds.

"I thought that was your job," he said, a look of confusion flashing over his eyes.

"I think we need to head back," I suggested, already steering the raft in the direction we had come.

"Go back? But we haven't found rescue!" Colby protested. I rolled my eyes.

"I don't think we're going to," The water was turning choppy and in the distance, I saw an island.

"Look! Is that an island?" Colby pointed at where my gaze was fixed. Growing closer and closer, my heart sank. It was our island. I didn't notice what direction we were coming from. This side of the beach had hard rocks, an area Nick told us to avoid. The water was rougher now, slapping onto our raft and threatening to overturn it.

"We have to get to the other shore!" I yelled to Colby. He glanced at me, wet hair covering his eyes that were filled with panic and nodded. We began to paddle harder. As if out of nowhere, a huge swell surged up from behind us, sending us barreling into the rocks. The next thing I saw before I went unconscious was our raft crashing into thousands of pieces.

I was sitting on the porch back home, drinking iced tea. My chair was slowly rocking back and forth and I was waiting for a car. Suddenly there it was, pulling around the corner. I stood up and waved to it as it pulled into the driveway. The windows were tinted so I couldn't see who was the driver. The car door was taking forever to open. I had an anxious feeling inside the pit of my stomach. Slowly the door cracked open. A gasp escaped from my lips and I felt them form into a smile. My mother sauntered out of the car with scratches, bruises and bandages on herself. She walked past me into the house as if I was the one who was the ghost. I followed her into the kitchen where she opened the fridge and took out a carton of milk.

"Mom?" I asked. She glanced up and my heart soared. She *had* seen me. But her eyes were someplace else.

"Hi honey, what are you doing home? I thought you'd be off at work," her face lit up into a tiny smile. I turned and froze. Behind me, a twenty year old *me* stood in the doorway.

"I'm about to go. I was just hanging out with Riley," future me shrugged. Wait, Riley? What was going on here? My eyes traveled down to elder me's crossed arms. A diamond ring was nestled on my left ring finger. I was engaged?! To Riley?! Was this what my life would have been like if my mom had lived after that accident? The older me looked sad, empty. Almost as if the void I felt in my heart from the loss of my mom was still there.

"Well, I filed the restraining order against your father," My mother said quietly and poured the milk into a glass.

"Mom you know that won't be enough. It's just a piece of paper! He's already done so much, what makes you think he couldn't do more?" I flinched as twenty year old me yelled at my mom.

"I know honey. But it's the best we can do," my mother said sadly and walked out the kitchen. The room took on a hazy quality and I felt myself drifting back to reality.

Opening my eyes was painful. I could feel them burning with bits of salt crusted onto my eyelids. Someone was shaking me.

"Monica! Monica can you hear me? Come on, please don't be dead. Don't be dead!" A voice pleaded dangerously close to my waterlogged ear. I groaned.

"Monica!" The persistent voice kept shouting in my ear.

"What?" I asked lazily, forcing myself to sit up.

"Are you okay?" The voice asked as I rubbed the salt out of my eyes. That was a creepy dream.

"I think so," A raspy sound was coming out of my throat. My voice. As the salt finally came out of my tired eyes, my vision went into focus. Colby's face was only a couple inches from mine.

"Whoa, Colby back up a little!" I jumped and inched back farther on the sand we were stretched out on.

"Sorry. I was just trying to see if you had a concussion," he pulled himself back.

"Why would I have a concussion?"

"You hit your head pretty hard on a rock when the raft when under. It drew blood." Colby explained. My memory was gradually coming back to me. I felt my head where a strip of palm leaf was wrapped.

"Where are we?" my senses were reviving.

"We're on the beach of our island. Nick helped drag you ashore," he shrugged like that act didn't hurt his pride. But I knew Colby better than that.

"Nick? Where is he?" my heart fluttered at the mention of his name.

"He went back to the other side of the beach where the rest of them are huddled," Colby once again explained. Man, what did I miss? Colby's face was easy to read. Almost like reading your favorite book over and over again, so much that you sometimes skip over the minor details. This detail wasn't so easy to skip over. He was frightened for me.

"So when is Nick coming back? I need to thank him for saving me," I glanced up and down the beach, hoping to see a speckle of black hair.

"You know, Nick's not the only one who saved you," Colby snapped, shocking me.

"I'm sorry. Thank you. Is something else wrong?" I asked wrapping my arms around my sandy legs. Colby sighed and ran his hand through his hair.

"It's just that I don't like seeing how you look when you're with Nick, or taking to him," Colby blurted out. Hold up. Was Colby jealous? Uh oh. I thought I had this figured out! I thought I liked Nick, but now that Colby was confessing...maybe I just need to think. Colby had asked me out, told me he liked me, and then kissed me. Gosh, maybe I wasn't the only one who was confused.

"Oh," I responded to his feelings. What more could I say? It wasn't like I had a speech prepared.

"S'okay. Don't worry about it," Colby stood up, pulling me up with him. His hands felt grainy from all the sand, yet it still made my stomach flip flop. Oh my god, I was turning into one of those girls that thinks it's okay to lead two guys on.

"Hey! Are you coming? We've got fish!" I heard Nick call as his head pooped into my line of view.

"We're coming!" I shouted back and headed towards camp. Glancing out into the horizon, a wave of sadness washed over me. Nick's plan failed. We're not getting off this island. I guess it was time to give up hope and live our lives there.

My hammock swung in the breeze, drifting softly back and forth. That was still not enough to get me to sleep. Since our huts were ancient ruins, we made makeshift hammocks to sleep in for the night. Mine was tied to two trees by the campfire. Caroline's hammock was right near mine, and we could talk if we wanted too. It's just that I didn't. She had tried to talk to me an hour ago but I faked being tired and climbed into my hammock. Honestly, I don't know why I didn't feel like talking. Maybe I just wanted some time to think. I needed a sign. A sign to tell me which guy is right for me. Nick? Or Colby? What if neither of them were right for me? Then what? Oh god, I would end up all alone on the island. Fire crackling caught my attention and I twisted my head around to look. Nick was sitting by the fire, poking at it with a stick. It was the sign I was looking for. I slowly got up from my hammock and headed over towards Nick, plunging my hands into my pockets.

"Hey," Nick said as I came closer.

"Hi. What are you doing up so late?" I sat on the ground next to him. He shifted to face me and in the glow of the fire, his eyes looked majestic.

"I could ask you the same question. I can't sleep. Being exposed out her, I don't know, it makes me feel vulnerable. Almost like we're being watched. It's kind of creepy," he dropped the stick and tugged on his growing out hair. I blushed and my knees turned to jelly.

"I get what you mean. It's an awful feeling, being vulnerable. I've experienced it too many times in my life," I sighed, looking into his beautiful blue eyes.

"Don't you wish that sometimes you could escape life? All the drama and decisions that come with it? And you know, just be free? At least for a little while? And I don't mean by drugs or doing anything like that," Nick asked seriously. I nodded.

"Sometimes. But I believe that wouldn't be fun all the time. I mean, if you escaped drama, how would you know who was currently pregnant in your grade at school?" I asked. Nick laughed.

"Seriously? That's what you talk and your friends talk about at the lunch table?" Nick raised an eyebrow and grinned.

"It was the main topic of our lunch table for weeks!" I smiled at the bittersweet memory.

"What are your friends like?"

"Kayce and Rachel are truly life savers. Kayce is the kind of girl who's all about saving the planet. She was responsible for getting recycling bins in our cafeteria. Rachel is more of a fashionista. She loves fashion and gives *great* advice. They're both really loyal friends," I boasted about them, "I've known them since we were in third grade. Kayce was getting picked on because of her Save the Trees t-shirt, so I stood up for her. At recess, Rachel came up to us, told me she liked what I did and gave us each friendship bracelets." I remembered that day so perfectly.

"They sound really great," Nick nodded.

"What are your friends like?" I asked, extremely curious about the kind of kids he hangs out with.

"I really only have one good friend," he started, a lonely stare creeping up on his face.

"What's him name?"

"Michael. We do everything together. Video games, scoping girls out at the mall, asking for their numbers and completely failing," I laughed. That sounded so *typical*.

"It sounds like you have fun," I tried to catch his gaze. God. He has such pure blue eyes.

'We do. He was going to Science camp this summer so we couldn't really hang out. Next thing I know, he sends me a letter with a picture of him and this girl who is his new girlfriend. I kind of feel replaced. Sometimes I question if he wonders where I am," Nick's eyes glazed over. Man, I so badly wanted to be Edward Cullen. It would have been awesome to know what he was thinking about.

"I sometimes think that Kayce and Rachel are organizing a search party for me, but they probably don't even know I'm gone yet," I hadn't spoken to them since two days before my departure. They came over to say goodbye, not knowing it was probably the last time they'd ever see me.

"That's what I think all the time. I used to dream that the prettiest girl in my school would be searching for me and then beg me to be her boyfriend when they found me. But, I guess that's just from an old crush," Nick confessed, a cute blush crawling up his neck.

"When we were on the boat, I had a nightmare about the boat stopping at an island and Riley would be sitting on the beach with his new girlfriend," I said. Had I just spoken that out loud? I didn't even admit that to myself. Until then.

"So you're scared of him?" Nick asked puzzled.

"No...I guess...no...I'm afraid of seeing him with another girl," I admitted.

"That's normal. Well, I mean," he chuckled, running his hand through his hair again, "I guess I shouldn't really be giving advice considering that I never had a girlfriend." I covered my mouth and pretended to be appalled.

"You? Never had a girlfriend? Impossible!" we laughed. A snore came from Bethany's hammock. That just made us laugh harder. And suddenly I was staring into his eyes. I felt myself leaning in and saw him leaning in as well.

"Monica," he whispered. Never before had my name actually sounded sexy. We leaned closer and closer, and then, our lips touched. An instant spark happened. Cheesy as it is, I saw fireworks. Our kiss deepened and my fingers twirled his hair. My insides exploded. I felt his hands around my waist and then I had to pull away.

"Was it too much?" Nick asked, panting heavily.

"No, it's just that I don't want to kiss you with everyone sleeping around us. It feels too public," I explained, hoping not to hurt his feelings. I wanted to kiss him again so bad, just not with everyone in ear shot. Plus, with Colby's kiss still on my mind, I had to straighten things out before I kissed him again. I told Nick I was sleepy and headed back to my hammock where to my surprise, I actually fell asleep.

The next morning, everyone started rebuilding our huts and I was sent to gather fruit. As I was coming back, I stopped short. A girl and a boy were in the woods, making out. As I came closer my eyes flashed with anger. How could he?! I thought he liked me, not that bitch! Now he's trading saliva with Bethany! I dropped the fruit, causing the mangos to roll out. Colby unattached himself from Bethany's lips, his eyes growing wide.

"Monica," he began.

"Don't talk to me," I shouted at him and headed out of the woods.

"But Monica!" he was still coming after me," Wait!" I spun around sharply.

"Wait? For what? So you can two time me? Go behind my back? Lie to my face? I thought you were nicer than that Colby. You're just another jerk," I snapped, my words stinging him where it would hurt the most.

"But__" I cut him off.

"I'm done with you," I said and stormed off in what I hoped looked like a dramatic exit. I should've felt something. Anything. But all I felt was hallow. Could it be, that I never had feelings for Colby? That he was just another hot guy?

When my feet hit sand, I collapsed. Fat tears escaped my eyes, rolling down my face. I tried hiding my sobs but it wasn't working so well. Oh what did it matter anyway? I didn't feel anything for Colby, he was a fling. My tears weren't for Colby, they were for home. If I was home I could have just hid out in my room. But I was going to have to face him every day now. It would be humiliating. I just wanted to go home.

I sat on the dry sand, my head between my knees, the tears slowly streaming down my face. Sand crunched under my sneakers and I lifted my head to see who was coming to bother me. Nick stood with his hands in his pockets. This simple pose made it become clear to me how much he had changed since I first met him. Muscles formed from heavy work that he was doing. They were there, just noticeable to me. In the sunlight I could see how his hair really grew out and created ear length hair that side swept on his forehead. His skin became tanner with the rays of the sun and I realized I was staring. I sniffed.

"What do you want?" I asked and featured my gaze back on the vast ocean. Nick sat on the sand next to me and put his arm around me.

"We're going to get home Monica," he said and squeezed my shoulder, sending waves of shivers throughout my body. I didn't let that distract me. I snapped my head towards him.

"Listen to me Nick," I said between tears, "no one's going to rescue us. No one's looking for us. We're just teenage castaways, no one cares about us." Nick dropped his arm.

"I care," he whispered. I shook my head.

"You care about me? Or about all of us?" I asked just as quietly.

"Both," he said even quieter. His hand brushed away my tears, sending more quivers down my back. I wasn't looking into his eyes anymore. He kissed me and I saw fireworks again. Oh, I was in deep trouble.

Nick is perfect. I don't know how didn't see it before. Maybe I was naïve, or maybe just plain stupid, but how could I have ever liked Colby? Nick is the one who makes me smile when he walks into the room, or sits next to me around the fire. He's the one who when I kiss him, I see fireworks.

"Hey Monica you want another mango?" Caroline asked from across the fire. I was too busy staring at Nick to hear her. That is until she hit me in the head with the fruit.

"Ow! Caroline! You have a strong throw!" I rubbed the spot where the mango hit me. Emilia giggled.

"She wouldn't have hit you if you had been paying attention!" she had a point. I shrugged, already over it. I picked up the mango, rubbed it off on my shirt and took a bite. You would think that after a month of fruit and fish, I would've gotten sick of the taste but man, I loved this mango. I ate the mango down to the core and tossed it into our garbage pile. I glanced over to the half built huts and grinned. Nick helped build those. I was so way in over my head. Caroline said that by the amount of effort we were putting into building them, we could finish the huts by tomorrow. I could sleep in a room again instead of a cave or out in the open!

It was amazing how the nights were as hot as the days. I guess that's typical island climate. I fanned myself with my left hand and swatted a mosquito with my right. An idea occurred to me.

"Hey, who's up for a little night swimming?" I asked to everyone sitting around the fire.

"I'm game!" Calvin announced and was already stripping off his sweaty t-shirt.

"Wait for me!" Caroline called after him, bolting to the diving rock. The others soon followed and I turned to Nick who was sitting across from me.

"I'll race you," I got to my feet, getting ready to run.

"You're on," he laughed, sprinting towards the rock.

"Hey no fair You got a head start!" I quickly caught up and used my new muscles to pull ahead of him.

"Oh come on! Are you on the track team too?" he joked as I reached the diving rock before he did.

"No, I've just always been able to run fast. Especially when I want too," I pulled off my sweaty clothes without even waiting for Nick and dove right in.

The water immediately cooled my body but when I surfaced and saw nick there in his swim trunks, I got hot all over again. That six pack that was faintly there before we were marooned was now defined. And he was mine. All mine.

"Monica watch out!" he called from above and made a "move out of the way" motion with his hand. I did what I was told. Soon, I heard a loud "woohoo!" as Nick jumped off the rock in a massive cannonball. When he surfaced, I burst out laughing. That cannonball had wrecked his hair so it stood on end all over his head.

"What?" he asked, not realizing how ridiculous he looked.

"You looks so funny!" I said between gasps. Nick smoothed down his hair.

"Have you ever done a cannonball?" he asked me. I slowly shook my head.

"Never?"

"Never."

"Well then, I guess I'll have to teach you," he pulled me out of the water, already running for the rock.

"Not fair again!" I shouted after him as I sprinted up to the rock. Once on top, Nick told me to stand by the edge and bend my knees.

"Now all you have to do is jump and pull your legs to your chest," he instructed, ready to do the same.

"Okay," my heart pounded in my chest. Being so close to him was making me nauseous.

"On the count of three. One...two..." he positioned himself closer to the edge.

"Three!" I shouted and jumped. I pulled my legs closer to me, just like he said and felt the wind rush past me. And then, I splashed. The cannonball plunged me down in the pool, but made my bathing suit bottom fall off. As I surfaced, I pull it up, and waited for Nick's splash.

"Yahoo!" he shouted like an idiot and jumped. I couldn't help but laugh. His splash skyrocketed into the air, drenching me. When his head reached the top of the water again, I asked:

"So how'd I do? Rate me out of ten," I giggled at his pointy hairdo. He shook his head like a dog and grinned at me.

"You did pretty good for a beginner, But," he hesitated, "I think you were a five."

"A five!" I squealed, already running out of the water.

"Where are you going?" he called from behind me.

"Do over!" I shouted over my shoulder as I raced to the top. No way was I getting a five for a cannonball when I usually got tens for dives. I heard Nick laughing as he ran up behind me.

The rest of the night was spent with cannonballs and laughing. I haven't felt more at home in weeks.

Was it possible to go from being miserable to being happy in a matter of days? Maybe. I know that just a couple of days ago I was upset and just wanted to go home. Now, I wasn't even sure I wanted to go home. I didn't have to deal with my father, worry about Riley and his new girl or even worry about what to wear to school every day. Sure there are some things I missed but if I had to leave, I probably wouldn't ever see Nick again. Or Caroline or Emilia or Calvin or Bidziil. These people had grown on me and right now, I didn't know what I'd do without them.

Days were blurring together. Was it Sunday or Wednesday? All I remembered are the number of days we'd been stuck. Thirty five. As I was lying on the beach, just staring up at the cloudless blue sky, I heard footsteps and sat up.

"Hey Monica," Caroline said as she sat down next to me.

"Hey, where've you been? We haven't talked in a while," I smiled. Caroline had seemed distant.

"I know. I've just been distracted," she said. What could she possibly have been distracted about?

"What do you mean?" I asked, tucking my hear behind my ear.

"Well. I like Calvin," she blurted out.

"Oh. I see. You've been distracted because of a boy!" I pushed her lightly, giggling, "Tell me everything!"

"Do you remember that night when he threw me into the pool, I kissed him that night," she confessed. A huge smile spread across her face. Was that what I looked like when I talked about Nick?

"He told me he's been wanting to do that since I talked to him on the boat."

"Really?! That's great!" I was truly happy for her. Hey, maybe we could double date sometime.

"Thanks. What about you? You've been distant yourself. And what's with the flirting with Nick?" she playfully shoved me.

"Um, well, I guess we're kind of a thing. I really like him. I talked to him when everyone was sleeping on the raft that first night, and I think that's when I fell for him," I felt myself smile.

"What makes him special?" she asked, lying back on the sand.

"He makes me smile, and I don't know, every time I look at him, I get butterflies," I giggled absently. Caroline laughed.

"That's how I feel too," she gazed up at the sky, "Do you ever wonder what it would be life if we found Nick and Calvin back home? Without the cruise?

"Yeah I do. If Nick went to my school I think I would've still fallen for him," and I meant it. I was falling for him. Hard.

"Mind if I join," Emilia stood above us, looking slightly uncomfortable.

"Sure," I scooted over so that she could sit between me and Caroline

"I feel like I haven't seen you guys in a while," she said, tugging at her skirt.

"I know, you've been hanging out with Bidziil," Caroline sighed.

"Partly. I've also been hanging out with Bethany," she said that name in a non-cringe way. If it was anyone else who said the *B* word, then we would have cringed.

"Why have you been hanging out with her?" Caroline asked, propping herself up.

"She's really nice once you get to know her," Emilia shrugged.

"Really? I guess you have to look behind the evilness and cruelness of her to see how good she is inside," Caroline said sarcastically. I laughed.

"Really, she's not that bad," Emilia protested, standing up.

"Oh please, she's just using you!" Caroline said. Emilia just looked at her, tears collecting in the base of her eyes and walked away.

"Caroline that was really mean," I told her, also standing up.

"I guess. But you know it's true," she stood up as well and looked me in the eye. I thought Caroline was someone I could trust. Someone who wouldn't talk behind someone's back. My heart was a heavy rock that just sunk to the bottom of my stomach. It seemed to me that I was wrong.

"Caroline, I thought you were different. You just hurt Emilia's feelings. People have to figure things out for their own and just by telling her that Bethany was no good, even if it is true, just made Emilia pull away from us more, "I stood my ground. Even though I was hurt, I couldn't show it, "I think you should apologize." Caroline sighed.

"I didn't mean to hurt her feelings. It's just that I've been in her position before. Thinking someone is your friend and then finding out that they're just using you, it hurts. I didn't want Emilia to go through that too," Caroline turned away from me, and I could see her shoulders shaking slightly.

"Caroline this "friend" what happened to them?" I took tentative steps towards Caroline.

"It was eighth grade. My best friend Brian had just turned into a hottie over the summer. Not like I cared, he was Brian. This one girl, who was mean to everyone yet widely popular, came up to me and told me she loved my shirt. We started hanging out and I got into the "in" crowed. It was fun, being popular, but I always felt self conscious. She would sit with Brian and me at lunch and for some reason I felt like the third wheel. One day, after soccer practice, I went behind the bleachers to pick up my phone that had dropped and I found them kissing. Not the sort of gingerly kissing, but full on make out. I could tell that they've been doing that for a while. Honestly, I wasn't surprised but I was completely hurt. Hurt that Brian didn't tell me and hurt that she used me. When they pulled away and saw me standing there, she even said that she only became my friend to be closer to Brian. When Brian heard this, he pulled away from her and led me away. To my knowledge, he never spoke to her again," Caroline started crying somewhere along the lines.

"Brian sounds like an amazing friend," I put my arm around her shoulders, immediately forgive her outburst at Emilia.

"He is. I'm so sorry. I think I should go apologize to Emilia," Caroline pulled away and headed towards camp.

"Tell her that story. She may be more reasonable with you," I called after her.

I plopped back down on the sand, once again staring at the horizon. It had become my new habit that always ended in disappointment. Although I had given up hope of rescue, there was always that little part of me saying "They'll come! They'll come!". Sometimes I thought they were looking for me, my dad leading the search party, never stopping until they found us. I pictured a helicopter flying over, my dad skydiving out of it to come rescue me. But that will never happen. There would not be a rescue. My dad would never lead a search party or go skydiving. Especially not if it involved me. When I was little, I hugged my father occasionally. But when I started seeing the bruises on my mother's face, arms and legs, and he just stopped the returning the hugs, they ceased. I shut him out. Sure, he was still my father, but he was just a figure in the background. A character in a movie, seen but not heard, that had their name at the end of the credits. Someone unimportant, yet meaningful to the past.

I was never a bad kid. I always followed the rules and came home at a reasonable time. But when my mother died, I started experimenting. I snuck out when my father was asleep with a hangover, started going to parties, being rebellious. It felt good. Until I was caught. Two months ago my father woke up in the middle of the night, just as I was coming through the front door. He was drunk. He began yelling at me, calling me horrible names, told me I was a sorry excuse for a daughter, told me he regretted having me, told me he didn't love me. And I took it. I took every word he said just because I knew he wouldn't remember it in the morning. When he mentioned regretting ever seeing my mom's ugly face, I snapped.

"Don't talk about Mom that way!" I screamed at him. At first he seemed surprised that I said something. But then he composed himself and gave it right back to me.

"Your mother was a horrible mother! She could never do anything right! Do you know why she died? Because she was a sorry excuse for a person and a bitch!" he got close enough that I could smell his beer drenched breath.

"You know nothing about her! She was a wonderful mom and I loved her! You killed her. If you were half as nice of a person as she was, she might not have gotten in that car that night. You killed my mother!" I screamed at him. I knew I was going too far, but this had been bottled up for too long. My father stood there, slightly dazed and then slumped to the ground in a drunken sleep. I stepped over him and went upstairs to my room. I cried myself to sleep. He didn't remember a thing. For the next two months until I left for the trip, I was more well behaved than I had ever been. I didn't want to go through another one of those confrontations.

By mid afternoon, I had become so sweaty from lying out underneath the sun that I decided I needed a dip in the pool. The campsite was empty. I could hear soft snores coming from the cabins. Everyone must have been asleep except for Nick. His face lit up with a smile as I came closer.

"Hey, where've you been all day?" he was sitting on a rock hear the pool, already in his bathing suit.

"Just on the beach. I think horizon watching has become my new addiction," I said as I sat down next to him. Immediately, his arm circled around my waist as he pulled me close.

"How about we go for a swim," he suggested into my hair.

"Okay," I answered but neither of us moved. My head twisted around for a kiss as he pulled me into a hug. Nick's hugs were protective. I felt as if the world could end right there then and there and we would be fine. I felt safe in his arms. Loved.

Nick smiled and bent his head down to kiss me. His fingers absently twirled the ends of my hair, while mine dug greedily into his mane. His kiss was deep, a kiss that was reaching to the ends of my toes. A kiss that was filling my heart with joy. It was mind blowing. This wasn't just some crush, I could feel it. My mind and body were craving him. I was falling in love.

I was disappointed when he pulled away several minutes later. But I couldn't help smile at the boyish grin that he was now in possession of.

"Wow. I never knew you could be kissed like that," he whispered. So he'd felt it too!

"Me neither," I said in awe. He just grinned brighter and pulled me to my feet.

"Let's go swimming before the others wake up," he suggested again and clasped my hand, tugging me to the diving rock.

"Do you know how to dive?" I asked him. He taught me to cannonball, so it was my turn to teach him. Nick shook his head.

"Okay, I'll show you," pulling him over to the edge, I explained that the dive I was going to show him was going to propel him deeper into the water.

"Place your feet and legs tightly together, good. Put your hands together at your chest and then when you jump, lift them above your head," I instructed. Nick did what he was told and waited for further direction.

"Okay. I'm going to jump. Bend your knees, good. Now watch what I do," I bent my knees and jumped. The wind sailed past my ears as my body dove off the cliff. I had shown him my swan dive, one of the ones I perfected. As I plunged into the water, I looked up, waiting for Nick. For some reason he looked a little nervous.

"Come on! Just jump, it's easy!" I called up to him, treading water. He nodded and then jumped. My mouth dropped open. He did a perfect swan dive, better than mine. How was it possible that he did that is just one try? It was almost as if he had been doing it for a long time.

"How did you do that so perfectly?" I asked him when he surfaced.

"It's because you made it look so easy," he shook out his wet hair, splashing my face. I laughed. His head submerged underwater and then next thing I knew, my ankle was being pulled hard enough to make me go under. The pool was clear enough that when you opened your eyes, you could see everything. I opened my eyes and saw Nick grinning at me. I had a sudden urge to kiss him, so I did. It was the best underwater kiss I'd ever had.

When we had to come up for air, Nick pulled me to his chest and kissed the top of my wet head. I had never felt safer on the island.

"Man, who knew three bananas and two fish could fill you up so well?" Calvin commented, rubbing his swollen stomach. Bidziil burped in agreement and then quickly blushed.

"It's a good think you're full. Imagine if we couldn't catch fish. You wouldn't be full at all," Caroline said, tossing some more kindling into the fire.

"Well, at least we wouldn't have to look at ugly fish," Bethany sneered. She was spending her days lying near the pool, sunbathing. And it showed. Her shoulders, feet and stomach were sunburned, making her look like a boiled lobster. I had tried to get her to put on the sunburn relieving lotion I found in the survival bag, but she refused. She said, very stubbornly, that it would turn into a tan. That was two days ago, and she still had lobster skin.

I rested my head on Nick's shoulder as he put his arm around me. Across the fire, Calvin and Caroline had a similar pose. It was pretty clear to all of us that they were together. Just like it was clear about Nick and me. Everyone had paired up. Nick and me, Calvin and Caroline, Bidziil and Emilia and Colby and Bethany. Bidziil and Emilia were still in denial about their feelings for each other but right before our eyes, they were slowly warming up to the idea. Maybe that's what the directors of the two week cruise for straight A students had in mind when they picked four boys and four girls.

I glanced up at Nick and he slowly caressed my shoulder with his thumb. I was itching to tell him I loved him. But would it ruin the relationship we were just beginning to develop?

My nerves were on fire. Nick was sitting near the back of the cave when I jumped in and holy smokes, he looked good. He must have borrowed a clean shirt from Colby since he was the last one to do laundry. We've been dating for a while now, so when Nick whispered in my ear to meet him here earlier this afternoon, I assumed I would need to look nice. I was right.

Do you know what sucked about being on a deserted island? Not having clothes that you could use for a date. I had to borrow the extra shirt and put on Caroline's shorts, just so he could see me in a different outfit. This was the night I was going to tell him I love him. I just couldn't wait any longer. But what if he didn't love me back?

"Hey, you look great," Nick said as I approached him. I laughed.

"Yeah right. So what do you have planned?" I asked him as I sat down and pushed a lock of his hair away from his brilliant eyes. Nick reached behind him and pulled out a basket filled with fruit. There were pineapples, apples, strawberries and bananas. I smiled.

"This is all for us?" I asked as he reached for a strawberry.

"Yes," he answered and lifted the fruit to my lips. I bit into the ripe berry and sighed.

"This is perfect."

"A great way to celebrate just being together after two months of being here on this island," Nick said as he dropped the rest of the strawberry into his mouth. I reached for an apple but Nick stopped my hand.

"Do you know what would make this night even more perfect?" he said and reached into his pocket. I gasped when I saw what he pulled out. Resting on a fine chain was a small diamond rimmed silver heart.

"Nick, how did you?" I couldn't finish I was so in awe.

"You know how you have your picture of your mom as your possession? Well, this is mine. My mom gave it to me when I was fourteen and told me to give it to the girl of my dreams. I kept it in my pockets ever since, never knowing when I would find her. But I just did," he motioned for me to turn around and he clasped it around my neck. I wiped a tear away as I faced him. No one had ever given me something so meaningful.

"Nick, I," I choked on my words. Instead of finishing the sentence, I kissed him. We must have made out for half an hour before I pulled away. He rested his forehead on mine, panting.

"I love you," he whispered. I had to hold back a new wave of tears.

"I love you too," I whispered back and kissed him again. He loved me! My heart soared with joy. Who knew three little words could mean so much? No one except my mother, my aunt and my grandmother had told me they loved me before. Not even Riley. I could see now that I shouldn't have been so broken hearted over him. Imagine if he never broke up with me. I would probably not even have kissed Nick. I wouldn't have felt like I just gotten off a rollercoaster. I wouldn't have fallen in love. I love him! I love him! I love him!

I couldn't sleep that night. After Nick had walked me back to the girls hut, kissed me goodnight and even said I love you again, I crawled into my hammock, ready for sleep. But sleep didn't come. I guess I was just so wired up from tonight that my mind wouldn't rest. I've had been wrong all along. Being castaways on this island wasn't a mistake, it was fate.

The morning sun woke me up from a dreamless sleep. I was the only one left in the hut. Why didn't anybody wake me? I tried finger combing my hair, hoping to get the sleepiness mess straight. I wanted to look good for Nick, didn't I? My mom always said, first impressions are the ones that are glued into people's minds. Always be prepared because you never know when you're going to meet the person you're going to marry. But that wasn't mattering to me, Nick's had seen me at my worst and my best. I wanted to look at least presentable after he said I love you. Can you believe it? He said I love you! It was like a perfect romance novel, he would say I love you and then I'd get all giddy and run to tell my mom. Except, I don't have a mom anymore. But I could tell Caroline. She had become my best friend here, maybe my best friend ever. I walked out into the blinding sunlight to find that Caroline was the only one around. Perfect.

"Caroline!" I called out and sprinted over to where she was sitting on the ground.

"Morning Monica," she said and tilted her head back to catch some rays, "How did last night go?" she was the only one I told where I was going last night.

"It was amazing," I sighed, my hand immediately gravitating to my new necklace. Caroline caught the movement and gasped.

"Monica! This is beautiful! Did Nick give this to you?" she asked gently touching the delicate heart.

"Yes, and you'll never believe what he said," we launched into a detailed conversation about last night and I left nothing out. Before we knew it, it was lunchtime.

"Wow, wow, wow," was all she said as the group came up from the beach with a pile of fish. I caught Nick's eye and grinned. He came over to me and placed a small kiss on my lips.

"Good afternoon beautiful," he whispered. I giggled and swatted him.

"Aww that's so cute!" Too bad it's making us all barf," Bethany said sarcastically. I rolled my eyes at her and took my place next to Nick around the campfire. I noticed Caroline and Calvin whispering intently at something and it occurred to me. We didn't know much about Calvin.

"Calvin, how did you get such big muscles?" I asked bluntly. Caroline and Emilia giggled.

"Yes, Calvin, do share," Bethany said with a flip of her obnoxiously blonde hair. Calvin shifted, looking uncomfortable at the position we were putting him in. He cleared his throat.

"Um, well, it's not very exciting," he started in his southern accent.

"We've got time," Colby spoke up. Calvin nodded.

"Okay, well, I guess it started when I was ten. I'm originally from New York. I lived there with my parents in an old Victorian house. My mom was very intuitive and believe that if she had a feeling, she should follow it. One day I was playing in the backyard with our dog Triton and my mom came out on the porch with a weird expression on her face. I asked her what was wrong and she said that we were going to see my grandma. She lived in Alabama on a farm in a small town. My mother and father packed up everything we needed to visit, but it seemed like a lot to me. We even took Triton.

"When we got to my grandma's house my mom and dad visited while I played with my grandpa's old toy car collection and then my parents were leaving. They said they needed to do something. They were gone all afternoon and through dinner. When they came back they sat me down and told me that they bought a house and we were moving here. I was shocked. I didn't know why we were moving and they never told me. After we moved in we were always over at my Grandma's house just talking. My mother never lost that weird expression. One night we were over there for dinner and my grandma just collapsed. The doctors said she suffered a severe stroke and pronounced her dead at the scene. It suddenly occurred to me why we moved. My mother had a weird feeling that she wouldn't be able to see my grandma again so she moved us down there. After my grandma died, my parents took over the farm and needed me to help. This was around the time I hit puberty so when I was normally growing muscles, I just accelerated the growth with all the work I was doing," Calvin finished up his story and the rest of us stared in shock, Calvin was wrong. It was an interesting story. By now, lunch was finished and I could feel the heat of the day bearing down on me. It was time for a swim.

"Hey, do you want to go swim in the ocean with me?" I whispered into Nick's ear.

"Why the ocean?" he asked, puzzled. I shrugged.

"I don't know, a change of scenery?" Nick nodded and we quietly left the group.

The water was slightly warmer than the pool but it felt good against my tanned skin. I treaded water and waited for Nick who was fixing his bathing suit. Suddenly he looked down and reached into my short pocket where I could see from here, a corner of a piece of paper was sticking out. I gulped. It was the letter. He grabbed it and wadded out to where I was.

"Why do you still have this?" he asked as the waves lapped our chests.

"I think I just wanted proof that it actually happened," I said, staring into his beautiful blue eyes.

"You don't need this. It will just cause you pain," he handed the wet letter to me.

"You know what, you're right," I crumpled the paper into a ball and tossed it as far as I could. Nick smiled brightly and then his look turned into terror. His eyes grew wide and he let out an ear piercing shriek. That's when I saw it, a shark's fin below the surface, just before Nick was dragged under.

"Nick!" I screamed in a high pitch I never knew I could do. Bright red blood rose slowly to the surface. I had to act fast.

"Help!" I yelled as loud as my voice could go, and then I dove.

It was a tiger shark and it and Nick were wrestling below the surface, Nick trying desperately to get air. The shark let go of his leg briefly and Nick swam to the surface, clutching for air.

"Mon__" he got out. I knew what he wanted me to do. Get out of the blood filled water and get help. But I couldn't just leave him! He would die. You know that feeling when the world as you know it falls apart? That's happened to me before. It's not something I want to relive, especially with Nick. Right now I was in a horror movie. A movie where Nick was the next character to die. The shark and Nick were closer to the surface, my body inches from the splashing and covered in Nick's blood. Suddenly Nick went limp. Instantly my reflexes kicked in. I began hitting the shark on the snout as hard as I could, just like I'd done with the oar. This only stunned the shark and that's when I stuck my fingers into its beady eyes. I heard commotion on shore, yet was afraid to take my eyes off the shark, afraid he would turn for me. With one final poke in the eye and a blow to the snout, it let go and swam off, leaving a trail of blood in its wake. I had to get Nick out of the water before other sharks showed up. Calvin and Bidziil met me at waist deep where I was slowly dragging Nick. They took over and carried him to their hut. I didn't realize I was shaking and crying until Caroline drew me in for a hug.

"Come on, Nick needs you right now," together we sprinted towards the hut and my dying Nick.

Nick's breath grew rapid, conjuring up a whole new batch of tears that I thought I had already cried out.

"Nick, you're going to be okay. Everything is going to be okay," I choked out as I clutched his sweaty hand. Come on Bethany! He was going to die without that cloth! The blanket underneath Nick was starting to get saturated with blood. I would use the blanket to put pressure on his wound but the blanket just wasn't clean enough. The last thing we needed was him getting an infection.

"I've got it!" Bethany cried, running into our hut with a long clean blanket. I quickly grabbed it and wrapped it tightly around his leg, putting pressure where I hoped the bleeding would stop. I bent over Nick, resting my heat on his hot chest.

"Nick, you're going to be fine, please don't die Nick, please don't. I love you," I whispered. Slowly and weakly, his hand came around, loosely clutching my body to him. This simple gesture, just made me cry harder. Who knew if he was going to even make it through the night?

Calvin, Bidziil and Colby were kind enough to sleep in the girls hut while I stayed with Nick. I couldn't leave him. I had to change the cloth every couple hours as they became soaked with blood. His forehead was slick with sweat and he was drifting in and out of sleep. I didn't expect to get any sleep that night, but somehow, my body gave up and I slept.

The lighting in the field was hazy. My heart was pounding. I was struggling to see the figure in front of me.

"Mom?" I asked hopefully to the vague image. The figure stepped forward. There was my mom, her hair cascading down her back and dressed in a flowing white dress.

"Hi sweetie," she said in her voice that made me want to cry out in joy. Was I dead? I ran to her and she opened her arms as I threw myself at her. Her hugs. I've missed them so much. She still smelled like her citrus perfume.

"Mom where am I?" I asked into her dress. She let go of me, something that I never wanted her to do, and turned to face me.

"For now you're with me, I came to tell you that everything is going to be fine. Please, hang in there," she stroked my hair, something that she hadn't done in a long time.

"But mom__" I started.

"Trust me. You'll be okay. I know things look low, but you'll get through this. Everything is going to be fine," started fading away, her fingers on my hair growing lighter.

"Mom!" I cried out. But she was gone.

I woke up with a start, her perfume still lingering in my nose. Could that have really been a dream? It seemed so real. I shook my dazed head and then remembered Nick. How could I have forgotten him? His brow was knit together in his sleep as I knelt beside him, but at least he was alive. He moaned and clutched his leg. He shouldn't be doing that. The pain wouldn't have lasted that long. Unless...

"Bidzill! Get the survival kit!" I screamed out into the early morning air. Bidziil ran in, disgruntled from sleep and clutching the survival kit.

"Look in the handbook for infections," I instructed. Nick's forehead felt hot with his burning fever. A clear sign that this was more than just a shark bite. He groaned as I slowly removed the blood soaked cloth, replacing it with a new one. He didn't wake up.

"Okay here it is. Infections: Replace cloth or bandage every hour and inject antibiotic directly into the infected cut or area," Bidziil read from the medical handbook.

"What antibiotic? We don't have an antibiotic!" I panicked, widely searching for the medicine that would save Nick's life. Bidziil dug in the first aid bag and pulled out a small syringe in a plastic box.

"Oh," I blushed, taking the needle and unwrapping the new cloth. His leg was swollen and bleeding. The shark's teeth left many deep bite marks, so not knowing which cut to put the needle in, I plunged it into the middle of his leg. I fought back tears as his cries of pain filled the hut. If my life was a movie, this would be the part when the heroine's true love wakes up and tells the girl they love them and everything's going to be okay. But of course, my life wasn't a movie. Life's a pool. You never know when someone is going to splash and disrupt your perfect balance. I watched Nick twitch and fall back onto the pillow. Fresh tears climbed to my eyes and I found myself sobbing against Bidziil's shoulder.

"Shh, he's going to be okay. Look," Bidziil held me and pointed to Nick. His bare chest slowly rose and fell in a steady rhythm and I smiled. Maybe life was more like a movie than I thought.

I stayed with Nick all through the day, occasionally accepting food from the others. Around one I guessed, Caroline came in and sat next to me.

"How is he?" she asked gesturing to Nick. A tear trickled down my face.

"In pain I think. He keeps making low moans but his fever has gone down. Although, the handbook says that if the patient has received their antibiotics, they should be fine within four hours. It's been past four hours," I tried hiding my panic. What if my mother was wrong and everything was not going to be okay? It was just a dream right?

"Maybe because he had multiple shark bites that it would take longer for the antibiotic to work," she suggested. I hung on that little strand of hope. I couldn't bear it if I lost Nick. I love him. Nick's head shifted position as he moaned. I wiped strands of hair off his forehead gently, hoping that I wouldn't wake him. If he could feel the pain in his sleep, I couldn't imagine how bad it must be when he was awake.

"I can't take it Caroline. I'm so afraid of losing him," I cried. Caroline put her arm around me as a soaked her shirt with my tears. I had already lost my mom, I couldn't take losing Nick too.

"You won't lose him," she comforted. I so hoped she was right. The island would be unbearable without him. Who would make me laugh, tell me they loved me or even kissed me goodnight? Who would brush my hair back from my face or have diving competitions with me in the pool? I needed him.

I stayed with nick through the next night, changing his bandage regularly when I noticed that the flow of blood had stopped. My heart jumped at the chance of hope. That could be it. It could be the part where he wakes up and everything is good again. A small part of my mind was bugging me about how it couldn't possibly happen. It just couldn't. I ignored the constant bugging and focused on the tiny glimpse of hope.

Early the next morning, I awoke to the sound of my name. As I opened my eyes I could tell it was way earlier than I thought. The sky was just starting to turn a brilliant shade of pink.

"Monica," I heard my name again in a whisper. I turned my head away from the sky to where Nick was sitting up. He looked weak and tired, but he was awake.

"Nick!" I couldn't help but hug him. His arms circled around my waist and for someone who was just fighting off an infection, he sure had a strong grip. I started to cry. My mom was right, everything was going to be okay. She had come to me in my lowest point of need.

"Oh Nick, I was so afraid I was going to lose you," I sobbed into his shirt, barely able to catch my breath. He pulled away and smoothed down my hair.

"You're never going to lose me," he said. His eyes were starting to close and I felt him slipping away. I kissed him on the cheek and ran out of the hut to tell everyone the good news.

When I got back, Nick was sleeping peacefully on his hammock without any trace of pain. It felt so good to get that obstacle behind us. Almost as if we could now accomplish anything. Even rescue.

Part 3: Revival

The days had become even hotter. I thought that wasn't possible. I had now found that I needed to jump into the pool at least three times a day to keep my body temperature down. That and drink lots of water. Nick was getting better. He was still weak, yet he could at least venture out of the hut. When I changed his bandage he had prominent scars from where the shark's teeth had punctured his skin. Nick hated it. I thought it was a reminder that we could accomplish anything. Nick was brave. He fought a shark and an infection and managed to stay alive. That ranked high in my book. I know that if it was me, I would have most likely died. Or maybe not. If I had Nick to hold my hand through the entire ordeal like I had with him, I could have done it.

Nick was resting in his hammock when I came in to see him with some fruit.

"Hi," I smiled at him and gave him a lingering kiss on his lips.

"I will never get used to that," he sighed. I laughed and passed him an apple.

"How are you feeling?" I asked him as I bit into my own apple.

"Better, I think I might be able to walk on it now. I'll be fine by late tomorrow."

"Nick can I ask you a question?"

"You can ask me anything."

"Why didn't you give in?" Nick sighed.

"I couldn't leave you behind Monica. You're everything to me. We've only known each other for two months but it feels like a life time. I would miss all this. Your face, your kiss, even your voice. I'm addicted Monica," he grasped my hand. Tears were welling up in my eyes. I could just picture the imaginary audience going "aww" at that moment. It was hands down the nicest thing anyone had ever said to me.

"I honestly couldn't think of what I would do without you. I love you," I kissed him again. It only took me two months to fall in love, but it was going to take me a lifetime to get used to the new change in my heart.

"Enough of this heart wrenching stuff. Did you hear about Bidziil and Emilia?" Nick asked me, a grin breaking out on his face.

"Only because Emilia sometimes talks in her sleep," Nick laughed.

"Bidziil isn't the kind of guy that just opens up about that sort of thing but last night while the four of us were just lying on our hammocks joking around, he just blurted out 'I kissed Emilia'. We kind of all stared in shock and then Colby said 'I knew it'," I laughed. I could picture the scene so perfectly.

"Emilia said in her sleep 'Bidziil has such nice lips'. Caroline and I looked at each other and started laughing into our pillows. Bethany was so out of it she didn't even stir," it was Nick's turn to laugh. I turned the conversation back to a serious note.

"Are you going to miss school and getting to do all the things seniors get to do?" I asked. I knew I was going to miss school. I was one of those brainiacs that kept to themselves. At least I had friends unlike some of the other brainiacs.

"Not really. I never really fit in with the crows. I just kind of floated outside the edges. Besides, I don't think we're going to get rescued in time for graduation which is what I'll miss the most," Nick chuckled. Somehow that sentence that was supposed to be taken lightly was heavy in my heart. Not rescued in time for graduation meant not rescued in more than a year. Would we even be able to survive that long? Nick was gaining strength, but what if another casualty happened. We might be able to conquer anything, but what if we couldn't?

"You know how at the beginning of the summer, you're just begging for school to be over?" Nick asked. I cocked my head.

"Yeah," I drawled.

"That's how I feel about this "vacation". It has gone on long enough and I want out," he shifted on the hammock.

"I've had mixed feelings about this place. First I hated it, then I loved it, then I hated it again, then I loved it and now I'm not sure. I think that once we're off this island, we're going to miss it," I shrugged. Nick snorted.

"I could never miss this place. The air is too hot," he used his thin blanket as a fan.

"You've felt the temperature change too?" I asked. I thought I was the only one that could tell the difference between the weather.

"I've felt it. It was cooler two months ago. At first I thought it was because it's summer and summer is always hotter. But then

I thought, that wouldn't make sense, you wouldn't feel the change so suddenly," Nick pointed out, putting his hand over mine.

"That's what I thought. Is there anyone on this island that's scientific so we could ask them?" I questioned.

"Bidziil," we said at the same time.

Bidziil isn't so scientific, but close enough. He knows enough about the land that he could possibly give us a theory. I approached him at dinner. He was on the beach, trying to put together a new fishing rod when I spotted him.

"Hey," I said as I came closer.

"Hi Monica, what's up?" he asked brushing off his sandy hands on his shorts.

"I was wondering, did you feel the weather get warmer in the past few days?" Bidziil furrowed his eyebrows and then stood up.

"As a matter of fact, I did."

"Nick and I were wondering if you had any theories on that."

"Actually yes, I do. It's probably just because it's getting later in the summer season," he suggested then went back to his work. I said a quick thanks and hurried off. I could tell something wasn't right. I could feel it. Maybe it was how Bidziil said it, or maybe I was just paranoid. It was a thought in the back of my head that was nagging me about missing something. I tried to put my finger on it, having no luck.

That night, as the girls and I were getting ready for bed, I brought the subject up again. Using my thin blanket as a fan, just like Nick did, I said,

"Whew, all this island work is really wearing me out. Does it feel hotter to you?" Bethany rolled her blue eyes.

"Oh please, you're being over dramatic. We're in the tropics, of course it's going to be hot," she plopped down onto her hammock, putting her back to us.

"You know, I think you're right Monica. I have noticed a heat change. Maybe it's because of the summer but I don't know. Something doesn't seem right about that," Emilia commented, slipping into her hammock above Bethany's. I nodded.

"Nick and I were discussing it earlier. What could it be?" I kicked off my sneakers and sunk into my hammock, swaying it a little.

"I don't feel the heat that much. I guess because I'm used to it at home. But there has been a slight change. I noticed that," Caroline said as she jumped, trying to get into her hammock.

"You guys are being ridiculous. There is no temperature change," Bethany scolded, rolling back to face us.

"If most of us have felt it, how would there not be a temperature change?" I asked. Bethany was just being difficult as usual. Man, she made a living on the island hell sometimes.

"Temperature changes happen all the time in Florida. There's nothing to worry about," Bethany tossed her hair.

"You know I think that this might be more of a five degree difference. If it was one or two we wouldn't feel it. But five we would," Emilia said quietly. It was if lightning had struck my head and given me an idea. The mountain.

"Do you remember when we hid in the cave during that storm?" I asked. Caroline and Emilia nodded.

"And do you remember how towards the back of the cave, it got just a little bit hotter?" they nodded again. I waited for a dramatic second and then posed my theory.

"What if the mountain is not really a mountain? What if it's a volcano?" silence hung in the air when I was done.

"Oh my god," Caroline whispered. I was right. I could feel it. That nagging thought had gone away the moment I thought of it.

"It all makes sense. A volcano makes an island in the ocean, so this couldn't be a mountain, it would *have* to be a volcano," Caroline said quietly. It was if she was afraid adding volume to her voice would cause an eruption.

"Do you think it's active?" Emilia asked from her hammock.

"With the heat, I think it's a dangerous possibility," I said, slightly panicked.

I couldn't sleep. After a long while, I finally got up and put my sneakers on. I already knew where I was going.

Nick was sound asleep when I entered the boys hut. I stood there for a few minutes, just watching him sleep. He looked so peaceful; I didn't want to wake him with our discovery. Not yet. I went over to his hammock to wipe a lock of hair out of his eyes when I tripped over his sneakers. His eyes fluttered open as he looked around for the intruder. A grin broke out on his face when he saw it was me.

"Hey, what are you doing here?" he asked, slowly sitting up.

"I couldn't sleep. Actually, there's something I need to tell you. It's kind of serious," I whispered so I wouldn't wake the others. It probably didn't matter considering how much they were snoring.

"Alright, hit me," he propped his head in his hands as he fixed his gaze on me. I took a deep breath.

"I asked the girls what they thought about the temperature changes. Emilia and Caroline agree that they felt it, Bethany denied it. Then I had this thought that maybe the mountain wasn't really a mountain because of when we were in the cave and it was a little warmer towards the back. We think it might be a volcano which would make a lot of sense. If it's a volcano, it's going to blow which means we need to get off this island. Soon," I gasped for air as he took in the information.

"You really think it's a volcano?" he asked, his voice barely above a whisper. I had to strain to hear him.

"Positive," I wrapped my arms around my shoulders, not because I was cold, but because I was shaking.

"We should check it out tomorrow. If you're right, then we *do* need to get off this island," he took both my hands in his. I traced his calluses on his palms with my pinky.

"I'm scared Nick," my vision was blurring as tears formed in my eyes. God I was crying too much.

"Me too," Nick kissed me softly, gingerly as if I would break. I loved how he could do that. But I wasn't in *that* mood. I kissed Nick back, forcefully, he responded in his varying pressure. Things were beginning to heat up and suddenly I was sitting next to Nick on his hammock, his arm around my waist and my hand in his hair.

"You do know there are other people in here, right?" A voice asked us. Nick and I sprang apart so fast, I fell off the hammock. I looked around for the source of the voice. Colby, who had a hammock above Calvin was sitting up and had a look of disgust plastered on his face. My cheeks burned. Not only was it embarrassing to be caught kissing, it was especially embarrassing to be caught by Colby.

"I better go," I mumbled to Nick. He nodded and squeezed my hand. I couldn't get out of there fast enough.

I watched the sun come up from outside the girls hut. The day was already feeling hot. After the kissing fiasco, I tried going to sleep. It just wasn't happening. So I came outside instead. Footsteps on my left interrupted my daydream of rescue. It was

144

the third most important thing on my mind and somehow it wormed its way into my thoughts. Bidziil was meandering over to where I was sitting.

"Hey Bidziil, what brings you here so early?" I asked him as he caught up to where I was.

"Nick told me about your conversation last night," he said as he sat down.

"Ah," I nodded. Of course.

"I don't know why I didn't think of that before. It's so obvious. Especially the structure. Look at it!" I looked.

"It has the classic volcano look. We've been so stupid. Colby and I are going up there today to see if we can find out if it's active," he said. My cheeks burned again at the mention of Colby's name. I really hoped he didn't tell anybody about last night. That would make everything awkward. I mean, I knew Emilia and Bidziil have kissed, so have Colby and Bethany but with everyone finding out about our midnight make out session, it would seem like an invasion of personal space. Not that we had any personal space on the island to begin with.

"I better start getting prepared, we have a long hike ahead of us," Bidziil said as he got up to leave.

"Good luck!" I called out, waving. He waved back and smiled. A sigh of relief came out of my mouth. Colby hadn't told. Yet. It was just a matter of time.

Since I was the only one up besides Bidziil, who was busy, I decided I needed to start breakfast. Walking on the beach in the morning after the tide had gone out was like taking a walk through a treasure chest. You never knew what you would find along the shoreline. As I was waiting for my fishing rod to signal a fish, I walked up and down the strip of sand I was on, looking for anything interesting. That's when I found it. A bottle was half sunken in the sand from being washed over so many times. I picked up and opened the cork top. A classic message in a bottle. But this bottle was old. The label stamped into the glass read faintly eighteen sixty-three. I gasped out loud. This was from the civil war.

Forgetting my fishing pole, I pulled out the faded grainy piece of paper. The writing was cramped, but easy enough to read.

My dearest Mary,

I am writing this to you from Maybreck Island where I am stationed. I am told that the war will be over soon and I can return home to you. I miss you so much. I know it is silly to write a letter in a bottle, but there are no forms of postage here. We are trying to cut off the Confederate's supplies and hopefully all will go well. I hope you are working on our wedding plans because the minute I get home, I am going to run to the alter and marry you. My parents still think I am foolish for running off to war when I am only eighteen, and even more foolish for getting married at a young age. But, I love you Mary, and I always will. I promise, I'll be home soon.

Forever yours,

Fredrick

Poor Mary, she never received this letter from Fredrick. They must have really loved each other. I wondered what happened to them. As I read the latter, I couldn't help but think that Nick and I might be like that. If we ever got rescued, he would go back to Virginia and I would go back to Wisconsin. Would we write letters like this couple did? If I ever got home, I would Google Maybreck Island. Maybreck Island couldn't be the island we were living on. It doesn't have any evidence that people ever lived there. There must have been an island farther away. I took the bottle and letter with me as I remembered my fishing pole. Lucky for me, it just started wobbling when I got there. I pulled in a big fish. Too bad fish went bad, the fish could have kept us fed for three days. Because we had no refrigerator, we couldn't really store any food. Any food that wasn't eaten, we had to bury, or it would go bad within a day. It seemed like such a waste. Back home, I probably wouldn't have thought twice about throwing away a half eaten banana. The island had turned me into a conservative person. Who knew? I laughed to myself as I trudged up the beach with the fish.

I handed the fish to Calvin who was in charge of chopping the head off the fish. No one else wanted to do it. Surprisingly, everyone else was awake. And they were all talking about Colby and Bidziil's journey up the volcano today.

"I don't get it. Why would we have to leave the island if the volcano is going to erupt?" Bethany asked with another signature flip. Someday I was going to cut her hair off. Nick sighed.

"We would have to leave the island because if it erupts, we'll all be covered in ashes and lava which would kill us," he explained patiently. I admired him for that. It was always hard to be patient with Bethany.

"But why would we be dead?" she asked, still not seeing the point.

"Because the lava will burn us you idiot!" Caroline burst. See what I mean? I sat down next to Nick, but he was so absorbed in telling Bethany why you would burn from lava, that he didn't' put his arm around me. My arm that was closest to him, burned with his closeness. I wanted him. No, I needed him. I needed to have his body touch mine in some way or I wouldn't be able to control myself. I was starting to get claustrophobic with him not touching me. I leaned my body into his, resting my head on his shoulder. There. That satisfied me. It must have satisfied Nick too, because he started smiling while talking to Bethany. That was something you could never do either.

Calvin had gotten the fish ready and the moment Bidziil and Colby were done eating, they stood up.

"I guess we should start our hike if we want to be back before dark," Bidziil said, grabbing his leaf backpack.

"Colby, be careful!" Bethany said and stood up. She locked Colby into a passionate kiss that even though I usually kissed Nick like that, I had to look away due to embarrassment. When she let go of him, both of them were unabashed. Huh. Must have been the overactive egos.

"Good luck!" Emilia called out to them as they started away, "Break a leg!"

"Not literally," Calvin called out as well, making us all laugh.

"So what should we do today?" Caroline asked, lying back on her elbows.

"Calvin and I were planning on figuring out some ways we could get off this island if Colby and Bidziil come back with the news that the mountain is indeed a volcano," Nick said gesturing to the mountain/volcano.

"I'm not going to see you all day?" I asked him, my heart falling. The best part about everyday on the island was seeing him.

"Maybe. Why don't you girls have a leisure day?" he suggested. I smiled at the thought. We could all lie on the beach and I could use that chance to tell them about the letter I found. I didn't want to tell them around the guys because it was basically a love letter. Guys don't appreciate that.

"Okay. You guys in?" I asked. Caroline and Emilia agreed while Bethany disappeared to the diving rock. Calvin and Nick headed off to the Canopy and I grabbed the letter.

As soon as I snuggled down into the sand, I took out the letter.

"You will never believe what I found in the sand today," I said while unfolding it. I gave it to Caroline, watching her face as she read it. Her face melted into a classic love face. Gooey smile, puppy eyes and a sigh.

"That is so sweet! It's such an interesting find. I wonder how their story ended," Caroline said as she handed me back the letter.

"Can I see it?" Emilia asked, holding out her hand.

"Sure," I turned back to Caroline, "If we get home, I'm searching them on Google."

"What would you look under?" she asked.

"Probably Maybreck Island. Maybe it's a historic place now," I shrugged. Wouldn't it be so cool to take the letter and bottle and turn it in there? It could be on display. Or maybe, if Fredrick and Mary had kids, then I should give the letter to them. It would make more sense.

"If Maybreck Island was historic, don't you think we would have read about it in history books?" Emilia asked, handing me the letter.

"I don't think so. There probably wasn't a major battle fought there," I turned to face the sun, dropping the conversation. I'll find out about it later. Right then, I wanted to daydream about me and Nick being in a situation like Fredrick and Mary's. Him, being on a different continent, me alone in Wisconsin. I would wait for him just like Mary did. It was a sign. It was a sign. A sign that meant Nick and I were meant to be together.

"Do you know what I don't get?" Caroline piped up after a few minutes of silence.

"What?" I asked lazily.

"Why is it, that we've never even seen a ship in the distance?"

"I don't know, I guess it depends where the captain of the ship wants to go."

"It doesn't make sense. Are we so far from civilization that not even a cruise ship going to the Caribbean will pass us?"

"Maybe. We only floated for six hours though," I shrugged. The heat from the sun was making me lazy. And burnt.

Caroline dropped the ship topic but launched into another one.

"So Emilia, how are things going with Bidziil?" she raised an eyebrow. Emilia blushed so deeply that her face looked like it was a tomato.

"Well, I mean, it's going good," she stuttered, blushing deeper.

"Are you guys an item?" I asked, squinting against the glare of the sun.

"I think so, I mean, yeah we are," Emilia continued on babbling about how her and Bidziil had a romantic picnic on the beach yesterday, and how she thought she loved him.

"Don't you think it's funny how we all paired up?" I asked, "We all found someone to like. What if one of us didn't like any of the guys? Then what?"

"I guess it would be pretty lonely here for that person. I have Calvin, you have Nick, Emilia has Bidziil and Bethany has Colby," Caroline shrugged. I figured out the lonely part, but what If we were stuck forever? Then we might have wanted to marry the guys and start a family. That would make things a bit awkward. I guess it was a good thing we had a mountain/volcano that might blow. That way we could make sure we got off the island.

"Guys!" Calvin came running up to us, out of breath and Nick slightly limping behind him, "Bidziil and Colby are back!"

Calvin turned and raced back to the campsite, Caroline and Emilia in tow. Nick held out his hand for me to get up.

"Why thank you kind sir," I curtsied.

"Your quite welcome," he bowed. We cracked up as we followed the others back.

Colby and Bidziil were resting on the ground by the campfire when we approached.

"Oh good, everyone's here," Colby said and motioned for Bidziil to start. He cleared his throat.

"Okay, well, Monica was right. The mountain is indeed a volcano," he said. A collective gasp went up around us. I looked at Nick with panic.

"That means, we need to devise a plan to get off this island. Now," Colby instructed, rubbing his neck.

"Do you think it's really going to blow?" Bethany asked, her eyes becoming doe like.

"Most likely. We didn't have to stay long. The heat at the top pretty much gave it away," Bidziil explained, "We have maybe three days at most."

"Three days!" Emilia shrieked. She burst into tears, forcing Bidziil to put his arm around her. I was probably the calmest one of us, and I was panicking. I turned to Nic, him seeing my panicked expression, pulled me away from the crowed. He took me into the Canopy and we sat on a hammock. Tears filled my eyes as he put his arm around me, pulling me close.

"It's okay Monica, we're going to find a way out of here," he rocked me. Just Nick's touch was comforting me. I felt completely safe in his arms. It was as if, when the volcano blew and lava poured out and hit us, we'd be completely unharmed. I know, it was silly.

"I love you Nick," I whispered into his chest.

"I love you too Monica," he whispered back, kissing me gently on top of my head. When he pulled away, I still felt the imprint on my head. Almost like it was on fire. I moved my head so I could look him in the eyes. He smiled his dazzling smile and kissed me on the mouth. I then became greedy. I moved my hands to his hair, twirling them in it. Oh my god, he made me want him so bad. I craved him. My heart surged to the size of a tsunami as I feverishly kissed him. I felt his hands on my hips, then the small of my back. Then, tickling my spine.

"Come on, let's go see what they've come up with," Nick whispered and smiled.

CHAPTER 16: 2 MONTHS AND 5 DAYS AFTER SHIPWRECK

My hand was clasped to Nick's as we ran. A flood of hot molten lava was creeping up behind us. I was out of breath.

"Quick! Monica!" Nick motioned me to come closer. I did what I was told and raced into his open arms. I was faced with that same safe feeling. A glow started to form around us and as the lava hit us, we were unharmed.

I woke up in a sticky sweat. That was one crazy dream. I pulled my damp hair off my back and wrapped it into a ponytail. A quick glance around the hut told me it was too early for everyone else to wake up. I didn't care. Sometimes it was good to be alone.

Turns out I wasn't alone after all. Nick was sitting near the campfire that was burning hours ago.

"Hey," I said, sitting next to him. Automatically his arm went around my shoulders. It was second nature to both of us by then.

"Morning. Do you know what today is?" he asked, a giddy smile already on his lips. I thought for a second.

"The day we get off this island?" I asked doubtfully. He shook his head and pulled me closer.

"It's my birthday," he said into my hair. I jolted back.

"Your birthday! Happy birthday! Why didn't you tell me yesterday so I could have at least gotten you a present?" I was on my feet pacing, desperately thinking of what I could give him. Then I noticed he was laughing.

"I don't need a present!" he opened his arms, beckoning me to join him. A light bulb practically went off in my head. Suddenly I knew *exactly* what to give him for his birthday. I snuggled back up to Nick as we watched the world around us come to life.

"It's his birthday!" Caroline practically yelled. I put my finger to his lips.

"Oh, right. But why didn't he tell anyone?" she sat back down on the diving rock where we went to get away from all the preparations. Yesterday, Bidziil had this idea. We still had the old raft form when we arrived on this isolation. The raft was currently in the Canopy being used to store our fruit and fish. The raft, which barely fit all of us the first time, could still float.

"Why didn't I think of this before?" Bidziil had cried out. I pointed out that since it was out of sight, it was out of mind. Anyway, the guys had decided that come two days, we would all pile in with fruit and blankets and head off onto the open water.

"All we would have to do is to follow the path we came in and in six hours, we should reach civilization," he explained, "It kills me that all this time, if we had thought of it, we could have been off this island."

Today, the group was inspecting the raft and finding other sources to put the food in. Caroline and I were glad when we could take a break. All this excitement was making me nervous.

"If it's Nick's birthday, why doesn't he want a gift?" she asked, popping a raspberry into her mouth. I shrugged.

"I don't know. Do you think I should give him a gift?" I asked. I needed her opinion on the situation, I just didn't want to give away what I was giving him.

"Well, if he's not expecting a gift, then it would mean a lot to him if you surprise him with one," she said.

"I knew you were going to say that," I whispered under my breath.

"What are you going to give him?" she rolled over onto her stomach, popping in another berry.

"I already know," I said and reached into my pocket. I pulled out a folded palm leaf that I had written on with an old pen that I found in my bag that barely worked.

"Is that a note?" Caroline asked. I nodded.

"I decided to write a message in a bottle. I'll use the one I found the letter in," I said, unfolding the leaf.

"Monica that's so romantic!" she squealed and squeezed my hand.

"I hope he likes it," I mumbled.

"He will. Trust me," she said.

"Hey girls come on! We're playing soccer!" I heard Colby call to us. Caroline's ears literally perked up at the mention of soccer.

I had never seen Caroline with that much energy. She was running and stealing the ball and making goals faster than any of us could even make a move towards the ball. The ball was a circular object wrapped round and round with seaweed, making it slip across the ground. The guys had shed their shirts and us girls were playing in our bikini tops. Well except for Emilia who was still fully clothed and panting. And of course Bethany wasn't there. She was still sun bathing. I lunged for the ball a couple times, only to end up with a face full of dirt.

After a half hour of playing, I managed to steal the ball away from Bidziil who was on the opposite team. I kicked it hard to Calvin, who scored by making the ball go through our vine net.

"Yes!" I cheered running to slap my hands with my teammates Calvin, Emilia and Colby. I of course, ignored Colby's hand. But Colby wasn't taking no for an answer. He wrapped his arms around me in sort of a hug. I immediately tensed. Nick was there in seconds, pulling me free of Colby's grip.

"Let go of her, Colby," he said in a voice that I never heard him use before. It sounded surprisingly sexy. Colby backed away, his hands up in a defensive pose.

"Okay, sorry. But don't you think she could make her own decisions? What if she *wanted* to hug me?" Colby said, threatening the already tensed air.

"I did not!" I yelled the same time Nick yelled, "She did not!" it was scary how closely we thought.

"Fine, whatever," he said and turned away. Most likely to find Bethany and make out. God, what did I ever see in him?

Nick put his arm around me and led me away from the group who were now involved in picking new teams.

"Hey, I was wondering," I started. Okay here goes, "Do you want to meet in the cave after dinner?" I didn't have to see Nicks' face to know he was smiling.

"Sure, I always like spending time with you," he pulled me closer and gave me a quick kiss that left me wanting more.

My nerves build up the rest of the day, my hands shaking as I tucked the note into the bottle. I climbed into the cave after dinner and slowly set it on the ground. I heard the sound of sneakers on the cave floor to announce his arrival.

"Hey," he said coming closer. He stopped when he saw the bottle sitting on the ground.

"What's this?" he asked, picking up the bottle and turning it over in his hands.

"Happy birthday," I whispered and pressed my lips to his, "open it." Nick pulled out the cork and unfolded the leaf.

"A message in a bottle," he said in awe and began to read it out loud.

Dear Nick,

I'm not sure how to put everything I feel into words. I guess to start, I can't imagine life without you. When that shark attack happened, I was so scared I was going to lose you. Yesterday, I found a message in a bottle on the beach and in it was a love letter from a man named Fredrick to his fiancé Mary. He was at war and couldn't wait to see her. It reminded me a lot of us. If and when we get off this island, we would be separated. You would go back to Virginia, and I would go back to Wisconsin. I love you, and I would miss you so much. Promise me that if and when we get separated, we'll always find each other again. I'd miss your smile, your laugh, everything. This necklace that you gave me means so much. I love you.

Love,

Monica

Nick looked up from the letter and gave me one of his dazzling smiles.

"You have no idea how much this means to me," he said and kissed me again.

I woke up around six a.m. I guessed. After I gave Nick his present, we fell asleep in the cave, worn out from the day. The gift I gave Nick had everything. Love, memorable and homemade. I rolled over to face Nick, watching him sleep. He looked so peaceful. He sighed in his sleep. Oh why was he so kissable? I could just lay there and look at him all day. His eyelashes fluttered, slowly opening. He groaned and stretched. Nick smiled when he saw me.

"Morning," he said sleepily.

"Morning," I said back, "Did you have a good birthday?" Nick broke into a huge grin.

"Thank you. I'll keep my gift with me always," Nick reached out and brushed a lock of my hair away. Slowly we stood up, brushing cave dirt off our clothes.

I poked my head outside the cave, looking for any sign of human life. None. Together, Nick and I climbed out of the cave and headed towards the huts.

"I'll see you in an hour or two," he whispered and gave me a quick peck, before heading to his hut. I sighed. He does something drastic to me. I mean, my legs went wobbly even after a peck! It made me wonder why people can't survive on love and love alone. I sure could.

I slipped into the hut, unnoticed. Or so I thought.

"Monica!" someone whisper/shouted at me when I sat on my hammock. I jumped. I glanced outside, expecting to see Nick's cute face peeping through the door.

"Up here!" Caroline. I moved my gaze upwards and there she was, staring at me, wide eyed.

"Did Nick like his present?" she was practically bouncing in her hammock.

"He loved it. It was perfect. He said he was never going anywhere without it," I laid back on my hammock and instantly fell asleep again.

The next time I woke up, I was the only one left in the room and I heard laughter coming from outside. As I walked out sleepily I heard a cheer.

"I win!" Bidziil punched his fist in the air.

"What's going on?" I asked suspiciously.

"Calvin and Bidziil were playing tic tac toe in the sand. Obviously, Bidziil won," Caroline explained.

"We've all been up since nine and kind of bored," Calvin said, tracing a stick in the dirt. Just then I heard a yawn behind me and saw Nick coming out of his hut. Man, was there a time when he didn't look cute?

"What did I miss?" Nick asked with the same confused expression I wore moments before.

"Bidziil and Calvin were playing tic tac toe," I explained.

"Ah. I see," Nick rubbed his hand against his slowly growing stubbly jaw. Even that simple move made me want to kiss him.

"So Bidziil, what are we going to do today in terms of getting us off this island?" Colby asked, speaking up for the first time this morning.

"Hopefully we can start adding food into the actual raft. The temperature I've noticed, has gone up a few degrees. So tomorrow will be our launch," Bidziil said as he surveyed the raft. I couldn't imagine that we were all going to fit in that. We barely fit last time but now we have everything else in it as well. Maybe for once, we were going to be lucky. The island had taught us something. We've worked together as a team, I've made new friends, and we've grown up. We could fend for ourselves, but knew when to lean on others for support. Most of us even fell in love.

"Do we really have to go into that rubber death trap? Rubber makes my hair go frizzy!" Bethany complained, running her fingers through her hair. Oh please. Her hair? Not again.

"Bethany you shouldn't be worrying about your hair! We need to get off this island or we're going to get fried," Emilia spoke up.

"Emilia! Worrying about my hair? Please, if anything, I should be worried about your hair and how it makes my hair look dull in comparison. Seriously, when *was* the last time you washed it?" Emilia stared in shock at her

"Y-Yesterday," she stuttered.

"Yesterday? Please, it looks like you haven't washed it since we *got* here," Bethany spat.

"Shut the hell up, Bethany," Bidziil suddenly said. We all stared, too surprised to say anything.

"What did you just say?" Bethany was more surprised than any of us.

"Stop. Insulting. My. Girlfriend," Bidziil said very slowly. I was shocked that there wasn't steam coming out of his ears. Bethany didn't reply. She simply got up and walked away, Colby following closely behind. Pathetic.

"Thank you Bidziil," Emilia said quietly. A single tear slowly trickled down her face. Bidziil quickly wiped it away. Is that how Nick and I looked? Sweet and innocent? If Bethany insulted me like that, I know Nick would stand up for me. Is that how Emilia feels? It was weird. I had known her for a little over two months, yet I still didn't know much about her. Before we tried to get off the island tomorrow, the girls should stay up talking, like a sleepover. I felt my face brighten at my new idea and headed over to Caroline.

"Hey, I have a plan for tonight," I said. She raised an eyebrow.

"I was thinking that us girls could have a sleepover," I suggested. I saw a sparkle in Caroline's eye That hint let me know that she thought it was a good idea too.

"Don't we do that every night?"

"Not really. We don't stay up late and talk or play silly games," I said. The sparkle turned into a glow.

"Okay! That sounds really fun," she bounced away giddily. Wow. When was the last time Caroline had been invited to a sleepover? Maybe it was her first one?

If I was at home, getting ready for a sleepover with Kayce and Rachel, I would be popping popcorn, getting a DVD ready and laying out pillows. Now I was just finger combing my hair and lying on my hammock.

"Ooh this is so exciting! What should we do? What should we talk about?" Caroline was bouncing in her hammock, making it sway above me. Yup, definitely her first sleepover.

"I know what we could do," the three of us, Emilia, Caroline and I, turned our heads to the person we never thought would participate in group activities.

"Really?" I asked, raising both my eyebrows. This would be good.

"We could play this game we used to play at my high school. It's called Fear, Dare or Truth. I know, lame-ass title. It's fun though," Bethany sat up on her hammock to face us.

"Let's do it," Emilia said, fanning herself with her hand. The air was getting unbearably hot.

"Okay. I'll go first," Bethany said, flipping her hair, "Emilia, Fear, Dare or Truth. You pick one." Emilia hesitated.

"Truth," she finally said.

"Okay, now I have to ask you a question and you answer honestly. Is Bidziil *really* your first boyfriend?" she asked, an evil glint in her eye. Emilia blushed cherry red.

"Actually yes. My school is an all girls school, so I don't really get to talk to boys," she said very slowly in her accent.

"Interesting," Bethany commented, "Now Emilia, you ask anyone else besides me Fear, Dare or Truth," Emilia turned to survey Caroline and me.

"Monica, Fear, Dare or Truth?" she asked.

"Dare," I said immediately.

"Okay, um, I dare you to yell at the top of your lungs, I love Nick Brady," she smiled as if this was the hardest dare in the world. I shrugged.

"Easy," I turned towards the door and sauntered out.

"I love Nick Brady!" I yelled as loud as I could. The girls inside the hut giggled. I turned to go back inside when it took me by surprise.

"I love Monica Jacobs!" Nick yelled back. There was a simultaneous aw from inside my hut. I could feel my cheeks were beat red as I came into the hut, but my grin was definitely showing off my feelings.

"That was so cute!" Caroline said as I sat down on my hammock.

"Yeah, well now it's your turn. Caroline, Fear, Dare or Truth?" I asked her.

"Truth," she said automatically.

"Hmm, who was your first kiss, and where was it?" I expected to get an answer like a guy named Tobey who had braces and it was at an eighth grade dance. Her answer was more shocking.

"It was actually Calvin. Here on the beach," she said very quietly. The rest of us were too stunned to say anything for a while.

"You didn't have your first kiss until you were seventeen?" Bethany broke the ice.

"Well, being a soccer player, my parents always made me practice. Don't get me wrong, I love soccer, I just wish that I had had more time for friends and boys. I've only ever had Brian," she explained. So I was right, this was her first sleepover.

"Okay, Bethany, your turn," Caroline grinned evilly. I didn't know she could do that.

"Dare," Bethany grinned back. The sinister smile looked more natural on her.

"I dare you, to run one lap around the clearing, without your skirt or bikini top," Caroline looked more evil by the minute. Bethany shrugged like it was no big deal and headed out the door. She threw her shirt and bikini top in a moment later. We raced for the door, trying to see if she was actually doing it. From the flashes of blonde hair running, she was. We whooped and hollered from the doorway as she took the last bend. Cheering on Bethany actually seemed like we were friends for a moment. But from when we tossed her shirt and bikini top, she flipped her hair and things went back to normal. Whatever that was. The game dispersed after that, but I had trouble falling asleep. The volcano was supposed to erupt tomorrow which meant we needed to get out of there.

"Rise and shine ladies!" Colby called into our hut, early in the morning. I blinked against the light, focusing my eyes. As I sat up, my breathing became heavy. The air was so hot! I felt like I was in an overheated hot tub.

"Come on! We need to get going as soon as possible. Get together your belongings into Monica's duffle bag and let's go! The volcano is already smoking. Monica, you and Nick are in charge of getting the raft ready," Bidziil instructed as he stepped into our cabin. I quickly grabbed the duffle bag, the one that had washed ashore and threw my picture of my mother and the letter I had found on the beach in it. Then I tossed it to Caroline and raced out of the hut.

Bidziil was right. The volcano had a steady stream of smoke coming from it. I turned away from the volcano and sprinted towards the beach where Nick was putting the rest of our blankets and pillows into the raft.

"Nick!"I called to him. He tossed me some pillows to put into the raft and we pushed it towards the water. The waves were low that morning, making it an easy getaway.

"I need to get the duffle bag," I said to him. He nodded, heading towards the campsite to tell everyone it was time. I grabbed the duffle bag by the hut where someone left it after it was full. I ran back to the beach, expecting to put it into the raft, but what I found was Nick on his knees. He was staring out to the water. His eyes were a book, with a sentence reading *we are in deep trouble*. I looked out to where he was now pointing and gasped, dropping the duffle bag. The raft was floating away, already too far for us to reach it. I wasn't kidding when I said it would be an easy getaway.

"What do we do now?" I asked, my voice quivering. I already knew the answer.

"We do nothing," Nick said. I pictured my dream from days ago, where Nick's hug had saved us from the lava. My mind changed it. I now saw Nick's hug and the lava coming towards us. Except Nick's hug didn't save us. Instead it engulfed us. I could see the end. All of us would die on the island. It was our death sentence. The ground shook as the sky rumbled with thunder. Problem was, there wasn't a cloud in the sky.

Nick and I started slowly making our way back to the campsite. The two bearers of bad news. If we had a third person we could have been the three musketeers of death. I felt tears prick my eyes and a sob, ready to burst out of my chest. But if we were going to die, I needed to take this bravely. We entered the campsite, Nick's arm around my waist and doomed expressions on our faces.

"Are we all ready? Come on, let's get off__" Bidziil stopped. He noticed the dreadful expressions and his eye widened.

"The raft," he sputtered.

"Is gone," Nick supplied. A gasp of shock went around the group.

"But that means are going to die," Calvin cleared up the subject. I heard sobs and turned to see Bethany clutching herself to Colby's chest. She wasn't playing it brave like I was.

"There's nothing left we can do," Nick said and started heading for the Canopy. Wordlessly, we all followed behind him, knowing we would probably never see the sky again. The ground gave a shudder, as we sank into various hammocks. Caroline was closest to the opening, monitoring the sky for ash, like Bidziil requested. It occurred to me, that she would probably die first. Once the lava hit the hut, it would burn. Leaving us with nowhere to go.

"This island isn't big enough for us to just move out of the path of the lava. The lava would extinguish everything," Bidziil had told us the day he came up with our, now failed, plan. Someone once asked me, would I rather die in the arms of my love, or die surrounded by friends. I chose the arms of my love (thinking of Riley), but who knew I would actually have to live both. I would be there, dead in the arms of Nick, within the short period of an hour or two.

The ground was shaking constantly now.

"The cloud of smoke is getting thicker," Caroline informed us. Bidziil told us that soon ash would begin to fall and that was what would most likely kill us. I tried breathing in fresh air, hoping it would calm me. But it only made me think of how little clean air we had left. There's a lot you think about before you die. All that life flashing before your eyes? It actually happens. You see every single good thing that's ever happened to you. My happy life was the one I spent with Nick. I could see every single day I've spent with him. But then, you see everything you're going to miss. There were only three things that I was looking forward to in the afterlife. One: Having Nick there with me, two: seeing my mom and three: never having to see my dad again. Abusive people like him have a special spot in hell. I noticed that the sky was growing a bit darker. The only sky was in front of us now, instead of behind. The end was coming near. I felt it. Birds chirped above, ready to take cover. Panic swept across me. How come they got to be saved, but we didn't? It was unfair. All of us lived only seventeen years except for Emilia and Bethany who were both sixteen. And Nick who lived eighteen years. I was supposed to be there, living my life on the island with Nick by my side. We would have even built our own little hut, maybe start a family. I knew everyone else would do the same. It was the best option besides going home. I reached over and squeezed Nick's hand. He squeezed back with equal force and I realized for the first time, he was scared too. The ground shook again.

"Still no signs of ash or lava," Caroline commented. It had been almost one hour. Maybe we were going to be lucky and get two hours. I curled into Nick's chest, wrapping my arms around him. I saw Bethany still sobbing into Colby, Emilia and Bidziil holding hands, and Calvin had his arm around Caroline's waist. I saw my friends, facing their deaths. Something I would have never thought I would have to see. Suddenly, Caroline shot straight up. At first, I thought she spotted the lava, making its way down the mountain. But then she ran outside to the middle of the clearing, waving her arms wildly. Puzzled, I started after her.

"Monica," Nick managed to get out as I pulled away. I stared dumfounded at what she was waving at. I began waving my arms frantically, shouting for the rest of the group to come out and help. The cautiously came out, watching the volcano all the time. I forgot about the volcano, focusing my attention on something more important in the sky. A black dot in the distance, headed our way. A helicopter.

My mother held onto my little wrists that were holding onto my tricycle handles.

"Come on baby you can do it!" she encouraged me in my ear. I put my feet on the peddles and started turning. My arms were shaking, was I going to fall?

"That's it come on!" she kept whispering in my ear. I felt her running behind me, down the driveway onto the sidewalk. The wind blew across my face and I smiled a toothy smile.

"Wee!" I yelled into the wind. My mother's hands left my wrists. I was doing it on my own! I started peddling faster and faster, using the handles to steer. I was truly riding a bike! But then, I hit a bump and crashed onto the ground. Tears started coming out of my eyes and my mother was there in seconds.

"It's okay honey, get up and try again," she soothed. I did as she told me and got to my feet. I planted myself on the tricycle seat and began peddling. Before I knew it, I was getting the hang of it again.

I guess that's how it is with life. You need to learn to get right back on your tricycle if you ever want to get onto your two wheeled bike. That's how the cruise was with me. I was doing fine, but then I gave up, and broke down. But, I got back onto my tricycle, and soon, I'll be riding my two wheeler.

The helicopter drew closer and closer. Soon I found myself shouting and jumping up and down. This was it. This was rescue! Who would have thought that it would take a natural disaster to lead us to rescue. The ground trembled again, signifying that this was our last chance. At life. Our groups jumping, shouting and madly waving must have attracted the pilot's attention. The helicopter was slowly descending in the sky. A cheer went up around me and I felt a single tear trickle down my cheek.

"We did it! We're going to be saved!" Nick cried as he spun me around, kissing me on the mouth. Hope surged through me, taking hold of every nerve in my body. I could feel life. I could finish high school, go to college, marry Nick, I could have a life.

The helicopter was closing in on our beach. Excitedly, we raced for it. I picked up the duffle bag on the way. I could hear the sound of the chopper. It was landing on the beach, the big blades blowing back trees, our hair and creating ripples on the ocean. It was a scene directly out of a movie. A movie I was glad to be in. The blades were still moving as the side of the helicopter opened. A man in a white lab coat stepped out.

"You're the group of teenagers who were on the straight "A" cruise aren't you? Why you're all over the news!" he yelled over the chopper's noise. We nodded.

"Come on! We need to get you kids off this island before the volcano erupts!" he called out, opening the door a little wider. He didn't have to tell us twice. We ran towards the helicopter and were helped on board. It was surprisingly big inside.

Besides the man who opened the door, there was another man in a lab coat and the pilot.

"Have a seat," the pilot said, taking off immediately. I shot an excited glance at Nick. I was getting my helicopter ride.

"I'm Dr. Murry. This is Dr. Samson. We're scientists studying the volcano," Dr. Murry said.

"Yes. This will be the volcano's last eruption," Dr. Samson said excitedly. The helicopter headed towards the volcano, away from the now forming cloud of ash. The two doctors buried their heads in clipboards, taking notes. I glanced at Nick, whose lap I was sitting in because there was no room on the floor, and he gave me a puzzled look. The volcano shook again, visibly, and I heard Dr. Samson squeal in excitement.

"It's a good thing we found you kids. Otherwise you would have been shish kabobs," Dr Murry commented.

"Well, we had a plan to get out of there before the volcano actually blew, but it failed," Bidziil said quietly. He wasn't blaming us, but yet the way he said it made it sound like it was our fault.

"You kids were very lucky then," Dr. Murry said, turning back to his notes. Dr. Sampson was practically bouncing in his seat.

"It's starting!" he announced. I turned to look out the window in time to see a small spout of lava, burst out of the volcano. Although, we could have still been down there and that was frightening. There was something magical about the eruption. The helicopter shook in the air making a light bulb on string inside the chopper sway. Electricity was a gift that I didn't think I would ever see again. The volcano only coughed up a small flow of lava, but it still got Dr. Samson in a tizzy.

"Looks like someone sat on an ant hill too long," Nick whispered into my ear. I covered my mouth to hide my laugh. But then Dr. Samson groaned. I followed his gaze out the window, and saw that the flow had stopped. There was no more cloud of ash, and the lava was already turning into rock.

"Well I guess that's it. That was the volcano's last every blow. Wasn't much, but it was something. The volcano is officially dormant," Dr. Murry said as the pilot circled around, heading for the beach.

"I need a quick break. Do you mind if we stop for a second or two?" the pilot called back to us. The scientists complained but, I was happy. I didn't have a chance to say goodbye before. Now I can.

As I stepped back onto the sand, I already felt the change. The air was cooler and it felt like when we first got there two months ago. I took a look around the beach before heading back to the campsite. The rest of the group was already there. I glanced at the huts before staring at the pool.

"How about for old time's sake?" Nick asked, coming up from behind me.

"What?" I asked.

"How about we go swim for old times," Nick suggested. I smiled.

"You're on," I said and ran to the diving rock, already shedding my clothes. As I waited for Nick to catch up-it wasn't long-I looked down into the clear water. It dawned on me. I would actually miss this place. It had been my home more than my actual home ever was.

"Ready?" Nick asked, already in his swim trunks.

"Push me," I said, putting my back to the water. He grinned.

"Okay," he laughed and pushed my stomach. Instead of diving backwards like I had done, I did a backwards cannonball, my face towards him. As I plunged into the water, I realized how much I liked this water better than a chlorinated pool. Water was home too.

As Nick did a cannonball into the water, I saw the scars he still had on his leg. It was his own personal souvenir of this trip, but I know I will never forget it. I was more terrified at that moment of the shark attack then I was of dying.

I climbed into the cave and gave one last look around. It was cooler in here too now. I found a tiny rock that would be perfect for my mission. I took it in my hand and placed it to the cave wall. Slowly I wrote: *Monica Jacobs + Nick Brady =Forever*. Cheesy, I know. But *this* was our place. And it always will be.

"Hey, what are you doing? The helicopter's waiting," Nick said, climbing into the cave already dry.

"Just taking one last look at our place. Let's go," I pulled him out of the cave. He didn't notice my inscription, but he didn't have to. I knew it was there.

Taking a final look around home, I headed towards the helicopter, with Nick's arm around my waist. This chapter of my life was closing, but another one was already going strong. I glanced up at Nick's face as we neared the helicopter. He caught my gaze and smiled, kissing the top of my head. Oh yeah, this chapter was definitely going strong.

"Come on love birds, we're waiting!" Caroline yelled out of the chopper. I smiled while Nick and I ran towards it, climbing into the helicopter that would take us back to civilization. Back to our lives.

"I've alerted the coast guard and authorities that we will be bringing you in," the pilot yelled back at us as we neared an island in the Caribbean. I clutched the duffle bag to my chest, feeling Nick's arms tighten around me. That was it. Our journey was coming to an end. The helicopter landed at a tiny airport on the island and someone pulled open the door, blinding me with what I thought was the sun. Instead, it was a camera flashing. Tons of them.

"Bethany! Over here!"

"Calvin!" How does it feel to be home?"

"Caroline! Caroline look here!" I wasn't surprised as the reporters and news stations called out everyone's names, even Nick's. But when they called my name, I was taken completely off guard. Who would have paid attention to me?

"Monica! Monica are you and Nick Brady an item?" one reporter called. I just stared, dumfounded. Bethany and Colby were already playing the relationship card, Bidziil and Emilia were shyly standing next to each other and Caroline and Calvin were just joking around with each other. But me and Nick? How did they find that out? Nick must have heard the reporter though. He put his arm around my waist and dipped me, kissing me full on the mouth. All the reporters started focusing in on us. I heard all the snapping of the cameras and the reporters yelling at their camera crew to get this, but I didn't care. All I cared about was Nick. As he pulled me up, three police men were ushering our group through the reporters towards a dark SUV.

As we sank into the leather seats, the car sped away. I finally understood what it felt like to be a celebrity. My lips were still tingling from the kiss.

"Isn't this amazing?" Emilia was in awe. And she was just talking about the snacks they had in the car.

"Look! Chocolate chip cookies!" she cried, pulling open the package and greedily eating them.

"I wouldn't do that Miss Emilia," one of the officers said from the front seat.

"Why not? Isn't that what they're here for?" she asked, her eyes wide in shock.

"All of you will be having a complementary dinner at the hotel tonight. We took the liberty of booking you all suites at the local five star resort here. It includes a dinner which is quite fancy. You will be meeting with your parents tomorrow when they all fly in. Don't worry, there won't be any reporters," the officer informed us. All of us stared in shock, and then cheered. A five star resort? A fancy dinner? It was all too much!

"Wait, but we don't have anything to wear!" Bethany cried. Of course she was always thinking of her appearance.

"Don't bother yourself with that Miss Bethany, you will all get to choose one outfit for dinner and two new outfits for today and tomorrow," the officer said as we neared the resort. We were confused why they were being so nice to us. You didn't hear about people being lost at sea and coming back to a five star resort. The officer must have been reading my mind.

"We don't normally do this, it's that you're just kids. And you've got parents who pay money," the officer winked. So it wasn't out of the kindness of their hearts, it was out of our parents paychecks. The SUV turned onto a tree lined street. Slowly, the resort was coming into view. I gasped as we drew closer. The resort was low to the ground, its walls open to let in a breeze. Palm trees were scattered across the grounds and guests were wondering around the premises. The SUV pulled up to the lobby and the officers came around to open our doors.

Stepping into the tourist crowded lobby, I felt like a hobo that just wandered into the Ritz hotel.

"Good afternoon everyone! My name is Rebecca, you're rooms are on the third building out back," an overly perky Rebecca informed us, "Here are your keys." She handed Colby eight pass cards. "I have it recorded that Miss Monica and Miss Bethany will be in the same room, Mr. Nick and Mr. Colby will be in the same room, Miss Caroline and Miss Emilia will be in the same room and Mr. Bidziil and Mr. Calvin will be in the same room." Each room key had the room number on it in big bold numbers. Colby looked over each key, handing one to each of us.

"Okay, this is where we turn you lose. Just remember, two outfits and one fancy outfit for dinner at seven. The car for the airport will arrive at eight a.m. tomorrow," the officer explained to us. He turned and then got into the SUV that drove away, leaving dust behind.

"Where do you think this store is?" I asked Caroline as we were handed a fruity drink.

"I'm guessing wherever those people who have shopping bags are coming from," Caroline pointed towards two girls who were loaded with shopping bags and speaking in a different language. Caroline and I linked arms and headed down a corridor. As we turned the corner, a row of shops emerged. Some of them I recognized from home, but others had foreign names that I wasn't even going to try to pronounce. Caroline and I stopped in awe.

"So which one do we go to first?" she asked, breathless. I considered the options and figured, what the heck? We were in the Caribbean, why not go for the local store?

"Let's try that one," I pointed two a small store that started with an A.

The store was empty of people, except one petit lady behind the counter.

"Welcome ladies! You must be the girls that were shipwrecked. You poor things," the lady said, coming from behind the counter. Was it that obvious who we were?

"We have been told you are allowed to shop. Would you like me to help?" she asked. Her eyes were bearing into mine and I nodded, knowing I would need to look good that night.

"Good!" she clapped her hands together, making me jump. The lady walked quickly over to a rack that had some different colored blouses.

After an hour, I hadn't found anything. Caroline had an arm full of outfits to try on for tonight and the two other outfits. I sighed.

"Come, I know the absolute perfect outfit for you," the lady gestured to the back of the store. She pulled me over to a rack with silky looking sundresses. She pulled out a pink and white flower pattern dress that was strapless. I think I might have stood there for a few seconds before I realized the stunning dress was actually for *me*. The lady thrust the dress into my hands and sped to the lingerie section. She picked up a lacy strapless bra and matching underwear.

"Try on," the lady gave me the lingerie and pushed me to the dressing rooms. Caroline came out with a light blue skirt and purple blouse.

"What do you think?" she asked, twirling for me.

"Caroline you have to buy that for dinner tonight! It's a perfect kind of formal. Not too dressy, yet dressy enough to be considered formal," I headed to the dressing room next to her, laying out my new outfit. I closed the curtain and stripped down. The bra, which I thought would be itchy (from all the lace), was actually very comfortable. I pulled the dress off the hanger and fitted it onto my body. When I turned to the mirror, I gasped. Was that really? I looked, *amazing*! The strapless bra really showed off my shoulders and tan. Pulling open the curtain, I saw Caroline in another outfit, this one obviously more casual. She was twirling for the lady and when she saw me, she stopped mid spin.

"Monica," she said, almost like a question. I nodded and twirled like she did for me. The dress fit me like a glove, hugging all the right curves. I turned to the lady for her response. She had one finger to her chin, nodding.

"Yes, I knew that was the one," she handed me some more clothes, clothes I had passed by when I looked and pushed me into the dressing room again.

It was another half hour before we finally left with our required outfits.

"I can't believe I actually bought a skirt! I never buy skirts," Caroline was saying. I nodded.

"Yeah, you seemed like a tomboy when I first met you." She laughed.

"I'm not, I just don't really like skirts and I chose sports over shopping."

"Should we go to our rooms now?" I asked as we neared building three.

"Yeah. I feel bad for you . you have to room with Bethany," she rolled her eyes.

"Ugh I know! I already had enough of her to last me a life time," I laughed. As we neared our rooms, I pulled out my room key out of my back pocket. The first thing I wanted to do was claim the closest bed to the window. Too bad it was already taken. Bethany was sitting on the bed near the window with a sea of bags around her. She was riffling through a BCBG bag, pulling out a short gold dress.

"I'll see you later," Caroline said as I stepped into the room. I closed the door, and turned to face the bags. Some had even circulated to my bed. I moved away Bethany's bags and put my own on my bed.

"You know, we were only supposed to buy three outfits," I commented as I pulled out my dress.

"I know. But I just had them look up Daddy's credit card so I could get more," Bethany flipped her hair and pulled out a bag of makeup. She sighed.

"Look. This is our last night together. I want it to be special, so truce?" Bethany stuck out her hand. I looked at it oddly. She wouldn't shake my hand that first day, but she'll shake it now? Hesitantly, I shook it.

"Good," she said, turning back to her bags. But I wasn't done.

"Bethany, why did we even need to call a truce?" I asked, crossing my arms. Bethany sighed again.

"I always felt like I was in a competition with you. I'm used to being the most wanted girl in my home town and school. When you showed up, suddenly two out of the four guys liked you. I'm used to all four liking me. From then on, I needed to be on top. I know, I was a little bit of a bitch but__"

"A little?" I interrupted.

"Okay, yeah a lot. But, everyone paired off, I don't need to be in completion anymore," she shrugged. I smiled.

"Well Bethany, could you maybe help me look good for Nick tonight?" I tried to make amends by doing something I knew she would like to help me with. She pretended to grimace.

"If I must," I laughed and finished pulling out my outfit for tonight. Looking at my dress, I knew I had to ask one more favor.

It was nearing seven o'clock when I put the final touches of my light make up on. A knock came at the door and I straightened my dress. I had taken the longest shower of my life to get all the grime and dirt off and I had brushed my teeth and hair. I was psyched to have Nick see me at my best.

"Ready?" Bethany asked, moving to open the door.

"Ready."

Nick and Colby stood at the door, laughing at some old joke. Nick, who was looking in Colby's direction, turned his head and stared. His mouth went agape and a blush crept up his cheeks. A smile slowly spread across his face and I finally said something.

"Nick? You ready to go?" I asked. He shook himself out of his daze and held out his arm for me to take.

"You look absolutely stunning," he sighed. My eyes locked with his, and if I didn't know any better, I could swear they looked right into his heart.

The lobby was fairly crowded, but I didn't stop to stare at the people who talked in different accents, or the cute kids begging for a stuffed animal from the gift shop. The only person I was staring at was Nick who looked completely handsome in his long slacks and blue dress shirt that brought out his eyes. We met up with Calvin, Caroline, Emilia and Bidziil in the lobby and headed to the Mexican restaurant.

"Are you the party of eight tonight?" the hostess asked when we entered the dimly light restaurant.

"I guess," Nick shrugged. There were eight of us and by the looks of it, all the other parties were of four or less. The hostess led us to the back of the restaurant, to a long table that was covered with candles. I couldn't help but notice that she kept stealing glances at Nick. Tightening my grip on Nick's arm, I gave her a smug smile. He was all mine. I knew he only had eyes for me. With Riley, it was a constant struggle. I had questions running

185

through my head that should never have had to be there. Did he like the new girl? Was he flirting with the waitress? Did he think that the girl in the corner was hot because he kept looking at her? With Nick, I didn't have to worry. There were tons of Rileys in the world. But there was only one Nick.

It only took a little while for the waitress to come to our table.

"May name's Katherine, I'll be your server. Wait. Aren't you the group that was found on the deserted island?" she asked, her eyes going wide. We all nodded.

"If you don't mind me asking, could you all sign this for me while I take your drink orders?" she asked, passing around a piece of order paper. I ordered a sprite and signed the paper. It felt so weird to hold a pencil again, almost like riding a bike after a long time. You knew how to do it, you just had to get into the swing of it.

"So what are you thinking of having?" Nick asked me as menus were set down in front of us. I quickly glanced at the English portion of the menu.

"Hmm, maybe the chicken quesadillas," I said, closing the menu. I needed to have some meat that wasn't fish. If I had any more fish, I thought I might turn into a mermaid and live in the ocean. Not that I actually believed in mermaids.

"Good choice. I think I might have that too," Nick clasped my hand and played footsies with me under the table. Although it wasn't working too great considering we were sitting next to each other.

"Guess what I'm getting," Caroline said from across from me.

"What?" I asked, turning my attention away from Nick. I still kept my hand clasped to his.

"Filet mignon," she said proudly. Just thinking of anything besides fish and fruit made my mouth water. A basket of bread was placed on the table and all eight of us dove for it. We hadn't had bread in so long. A good thing that came out of the trip was that it taught me to value the small things. Like bread.

When the waitress brought us our food, I couldn't help but stare at the oversized portions. How in the world was I supposed to eat it? I gave Nick and Caroline a quizzical look and dug in. Then I realized why the portions were so big. The kitchen probably had so many people ordering seconds they were so good! The cheese melted in my mouth while the chicken had a smoky taste with juicy peppers and soft tortillas. I was making myself hungry just by thinking about what I was eating. I gave a contented sigh out loud. Eating food like that felt like I hadn't eaten in weeks. Well, then again, I didn't eat *much* in weeks. On my plate were five fat quesadillas. By the time we were halfway through our dinner, there were three of them. Yup, they were that big.

"I can't believe this is really over," Emilia quietly said. I nodded.

"I know. It feels like just yesterday we got on that doomed boat," I took a sip of my Sprite. Who knew carbonated bubbles could make a person feel so happy?

"Yeah. It feels good to be back in civilization though," Calvin said around the enchilada he was eating.

"I'm glad to be going home," Caroline sighed.

"Me too. But we all have to stay in touch," Colby commented. That's right. We weren't going to see each other every day and we all lived hundreds of miles apart from each other. I would be going back to Wisconsin, Nick to Virginia, Caroline to California, Colby to Colorado, Calvin to Alabama, Bidziil to Washington, Emilia to Maine and Bethany to Florida. We were going to be spread out on all four corners of the U.S. and I would be far away from Nick. It was our last night together and hopefully Bethany had set up everything as my favor. I reached into my bag for a pen and a tablet I had stuck in there earlier.

"Here, everyone should write down their e-mails and phone numbers," I handed a piece of paper to Emilia who was sitting next to me while handing Nick the rest of the tablet. I quickly jotted down my e-mail and cell number and added a smiley face on Caroline's paper before grabbing the next one.

I looked at the e-mail and numbers of friends I knew I would have forever. And yes, I considered Bethany and Colby friends. I had to stay in touch with these people, they were the friends that stayed with you through the thick and the thin. Literally.

"What do you think happened to the crew that deserted us?" I asked. The thought had been playing in my mind since we landed on the island.

"I heard from some of the hotel staff that they are getting put out of business. Apparently Diane is testifying against them. Good riddance. We don't need any more teenagers lost at sea," Calvin said.

"Is everyone ready for dessert?" Katherine came back just as we finished eating the scrapes of food on our plates.

"I think we are," Caroline nodded, pointing to the menu, "We would all like to split the chocolate cake." Chocolate. Another thing that I always took for granted. And another thing I had desperately missed.

"I think I'll miss the days on the island when it was just the eight of us," I said.

"It was a good run," Calvin agreed.

"An awesome adventure," Colby commented.

"One that will never be forgotten," Nick nodded.

"To friends," Bidziil toasted, raising his glass. I did the same.

"To new discoveries," Caroline said, looking at Calvin.

"To life," Emilia raised her glass.

"To us, teenage castaways," I said smiling.

The chocolate cake must have been the richest on Earth. Of course, the boys devoured it, but us girls could only eat so much. Chocolate was only good in small doses. Just like Bethany. You had to admit though, she made quite an impression so she'll never be forgotten. I looked around the table at everyone. We had changed so much. Not only physically (cough-cough-Bidziil-Nick-cough-cough) but emotionally as well. I think we all grew up a little. Bethany seemed a tad more intelligent, Colby a little more aware that the world didn't revolve around him, and me, I was open. After my mom's death I shut myself away. But coming to the island, I actually talked about my mom's death in what felt like forever. I didn't hide myself away. I let people in. We had all changed for the better.

"Will there be anything else tonight?" Katherine asked, handing us the receipt. Everything had been charged to the room. We obviously weren't paying for it.

"No, thank you," Emilia replied as we stood to go. We headed out of the restaurant towards building three. We were laughing and talking as we neared our rooms. None of us wanted to say goodnight to anyone. Finally Caroline yawned and she and Emilia headed off to their room. Calvin and Bidziil soon followed. And then it was me, Nick, Colby and Bethany. Bethany gave me a small wink to let me know our plan was about to go into action.

"Hey Colby, why don't we share a room tonight," she whispered into his ear loud enough for Nick and I to hear.

"Well, I'm sharing a room with Nick so," he didn't finish.

"Oh of course! Well Monica would be totally fine with it. Come on Colby," she pulled a non-hesitant Colby across the hall, leaving Nick and I alone.

"Well that was odd," he finally said, smiling.

"No it wasn't," I grinned. He raised an eyebrow and I reached for my key. I didn't say a word as I pulled him in for a kiss. I softly closed the door behind us.

"Did you and Nick have fun last night?" Bethany asked as we began putting our new clothes into cheap suitcases that were supplied for us. I blushed.

"Yeah, we did," I didn't really want to talk about my love life. Especially with Bethany. Sure, she was better than she was at the beginning of the journey, but she was still Bethany.

"Colby and I had fun too. It's a good think I already went through all the guy at my school," Bethany shrugged.

"What do you mean?" I asked slowly.

"I mean that I've already dated all the good looking guys in my school so now I have a new guy. If I had a couple more guys to date, I might have already dropped Colby like a hot potato," she zipped her suitcase and turned to face me. Was Bethany really that shallow to drop a guy because another guy was available? She looked up from her bag and saw my confused face. She laughed.

"I'm just kidding Monica, chill. I really do like Colby," well at least she was kidding. I grabbed my suitcase and headed towards the door. In approximately six hours I would be on a plane home. Everyone had to be at the airport two hours before their plane. But since our parents were flying in, we needed to be there four hours early. My plane was coming a little later.

I pulled open our hotel door and rolled my suitcase down the hallway towards the entrance of building three. In the lobby,

Bethany and I caught up with the others. Nick gave me a quick kiss.

"PDA much?" Bethany smirked and turned to suck face with Colby.

"You're one to talk," I rolled my eyes. Same old Bethany. I turned to Emilia who was crying on Bidziil's shoulder.

"I can't believe we're all separating," she sobbed.

"Don't worry Emilia, we'll keep in touch," Caroline patted her shoulder. I wasn't sure, but I could swear I saw Caroline wipe a tear from her eye.

"We're ready for your bags," an officer approached us. It was a different one from yesterday but he still had the formal attitude towards us. We all handed our bags in and watched him load up the SUV. Bethany climbed in first, followed by Colby. Nick and I were the last in. For some reason, I didn't want to leave.

The ride to the airport was long. But I didn't mind. It meant that I had more time with Nick. A delay in our goodbye. Caroline and I played Poker with a deck of cards we found in the car and I cuddled with Nick. He and Colby were discussing which felt hotter in august, Colorado or Virginia. When I began seeing signs for the larger airport on the island, I felt myself begin to break down. But I couldn't cry. Not here, not now.

The SUV pulled up to an empty parking spot near the entrance. The officer helped us out of the vehicle and handed us our bags and tickets.

"Follow me please," he led us through the mass of people, all tourists. You could tell by them huddling together, taking pictures or by their overstuffed suitcases. Or even by the shrieks of "I can't believe we're here!". The officer led us up to terminal B where our parent's planes would be coming in. I wasn't excited. I didn't want to go home to my drunken dad, live in the house knowing that was the last place my mom had ever wanted to be. I wished I could go with Nick. Sure, he didn't have a perfect life either, but then we'd be together and I wouldn't be haunted with memories of my past. Caroline and I sat in the overstuffed chairs that were supplied for travelers.

"I can't believe my parents are going to be here soon," she sighed, "It'll be nice getting home, preparing for school and seeing friends again." I nodded. It would be nice preparing for school and seeing friends again, I just wasn't looking forward to the getting home part. It didn't even feel like home anymore.

"I'm going to miss you Caroline," I chocked. Great. My throat was closing up and my eyes were filling with tears. Once I start crying, I can't stop.

"I'm going to miss you too. I think you're the best friend I've ever had," she wiped her eyes.

"Oh my god! Emilia!" a woman's high pitched British voice came through the terminal. A lady with Emilia's jet black hair came running towards her, throwing herself in Emilia's arms.

"Mum! I've missed you so much!" Emilia began sobbing. I watched as two girls followed Emilia's mom. They must have been Veronica and Georgia. They were adorable. I noticed more parents were running and hugging their kids. Bidziil's parents, Calvin's, Bethany's, Colby's and then Caroline shrieked. She ran towards two people in business suites. Caroline had her mother's curly brown hair and her dad's athletic build. They both smiled and hugged Caroline in unison. Soon, it was only Nick and I who were parentless.

"Where are your parents?" I asked him as he sat down next to me.

"They had to come on a later flight since they're coming from France," he explained, "What about your dad?"

"Coming on a later flight. Apparently there weren't that many flights going to the Caribbean from Wisconsin," I rolled my eyes.

"So I guess we're stuck together," he smiled, making his blue eyes twinkle.

"Yeah, I guess we are," I sighed. There was nothing wrong with being stuck with Nick. In fact, I would chose to be stuck with Nick every day of my life.

"No mum! No!" my head snapped towards where Emilia was crying out. Her mother had her by the arm, trying to drag her away from Bidziil.

"Emilia, you knew the rules! No dating until you're eighteen!" her mother shouted to her.

"But that's not fair! I love him! Let me go!" Emilia shouted back.

"Absolutely not," her mother took the two younger girls by the hand and stormed off to talk to the rest of the parents. Nick and I approached the group.

"I can't believe I'm the first person to leave," she sobbed, "Promise we'll stay in touch." She addressed all of us. I pulled her in for a hug, a tear rolling down her cheek. Emilia pulled away and hugged everyone else. But when she got to Bidziil he said,

"Oh what the heck," and kissed her. Emilia's mother stormed back over and ripped her from Bidziil's embrace. It was a scene out of a movie as her mother pulled her through the airport and Emilia shouting back,

"Bidziil I love you!"

The rest of us were beginning to drop like flies. Calvin was the next to leave, him kissing Caroline on the cheek before heading to his plane with his parents, leaving behind Caroline who was still touching the place where he kissed her. Then it was Bidziil who I gave a hug to. Next it was Bethany who just waved to everyone and planted a huge kiss on Colby's lips. A flight attendant announced that flight two eighty nine will be boarding to California shortly.

"Well, that's my ride. My parents are waiting for me," Caroline said as she grabbed her bag. Tears were rapidly rolling down my face.

"Caroline, please stay in touch," I said as I hugged her.

"I will. But promise *me* that you and Nick will stay together," she said, turning to hug Nick.

"Why would you ask me to promise that?" I asked, even though I knew I wouldn't have any trouble keeping that promise.

"Because. You two are perfect for each other. If you two can't stay together, than where is the hope for the rest of us?" she asked, walking backwards to her parents. I waved goodbye to my best friend and watched her head to her plane. Then I was left with the two guys who I was once in a twisted love triangle with.

I could feel the tension in the air. I wanted to say goodbye to Colby, I really did. Putting aside everything that had happened with him, he was a good friend. To ease the tension, I asked the officer near us what would happen to the island.

"The island? Well, since the volcano is now dormant, It's going to be turned into a resort. It's going to be called Castaway Island," the officer answered and then turned back to the newspaper he was reading.

"A resort huh? That would give us an excuse to visit," Colby said and winked. His plane was called and before I could react, he pulled me into a hug.

"Take care Monica," he whispered, already heading off towards his plane. He didn't look back.

I curled up against Nick on the terminal chairs.

"Promise me you'll e-mail me every day," I said to him. He smiled down at me.

"I'll do that and I'll call. Maybe even text," he said, pulling me closer.

"Don't text. I'd rather hear your voice." How was I going to get through my senior year without him? At least I wouldn't have to worry about Riley now. I didn't care if he ended up with dating thousands of girls. I'll have Nick, not him. And I'm glad. I heard footsteps behind me, then a deep male's voice.

"Monica?" he asked. I turned around slowly. There he was. My dad. Standing next to a woman that was wearing too tight clothing and who I didn't recognize at all.

"Hi honey," my dad said to me, reaching out for a hug as I stood up. I stood stiffly, not willing to return his hug.

"Okay then," he said and then turned to the women.

"Monica, this is your new mother."

My world swirled, noises blurring together as I stared in horror. I had been missing for two and a half months and *this* has been what was going on?

"It's so nice to meet you, I can tell we'll be great friends," the women, my new *stepmom* said in a too high pitched voice. I didn't say anything and turned to my Dad.

"How could you do this to me?!" I yelled at him. He stared at me like I should be happy for him instead of mad.

"Look Monica__" he started. I didn't let him finish.

"I was *missing* for two months! You didn't even care did you? You were happy to get rid of me so you could go get hitched to this hooker? You should be ashamed. You're the one who killed my mom. You abused her! That's what led her to driving off too fast and getting killed in a car accident. It was because of you!" I yelled at him. It happened so fast I didn't see it coming until I was on the ground holding my cheek where he slapped me. Nick was on him in a instant.

"Don't ever touch her," he growled. I hadn't seen him this angry since, well, never.

"Who do you think you are?" my dad spat at him.

"Her boyfriend. The only man that loves her," he shot back, releasing my dad from where he had him by the shirt. Suddenly I realized I couldn't live with him. I couldn't. If I did, I would surely end up like my mom. Dead. Or worse. There was only one place I could go and I don't know why I didn't think of this before. My Grandmother's house was close enough that I could stay in the same school district, but far enough away from my father. Nick bent down next to me and helped me to my feet. I turned on my dad.

"If you think I'm coming home to live with you, you're wrong. The minute we land in Wisconsin, I'm going to live at Grandma's," I said and grabbed my bag, heading to the farthest corner of the gate. Nick, of course, followed me.

"Monica, I'm so sorry," he said as tears began dashing down my face again. This time though, they weren't for goodbyes, they were for new beginnings.

"Nick darling!" a tall blonde woman approached us, kissing Nick on both cheeks. A man with salt and pepper hair stood behind her.

"Hi dad, hi Laura," Nick said in a monotone voice. His dad waved limply.

"Nick who's this? A little friend?" Laura asked, looking me up and down. She slightly lifted her nose up at me. Great, a grown-up Bethany.

"Laura, dad, this is my girlfriend Monica," he put his arm around my waist and I blushed. His dad raised his eye brows but it was Laura who said what he was thinking.

"Oh! Nick are you sure? She doesn't seem like your type," Laura was making it pretty clear that she thought I wasn't good enough for him.

"Yes, I'm positive," Nick said, tightening his grip. Laura caught sight of his shark scars on his leg.

"Oh my, Nick! What happened to your leg?" she gasped. Nick shrugged.

"It's a long story."

"Well, Nick we'll let you make your goodbyes. We'll meet you at the gate," Laura said and ruffled his hair. Nick quickly reached up to straighten it. Once they were gone, I turned to him.

"They seem nice," I said sarcastically. He shrugged.

"Laura is the kind of person who has to have everything a certain way. Including my life. My dad doesn't say much and basically agrees with everything she says. That's probably how I ended up going on this trip," Nick said, squeezing me tight. We walked hand in hand over to his gate.

"Monica, I am going to miss you so much," Nick said, smiling sadly at me. That one smile opened up the floodgates again. Nick pressed me against his shoulder as I sobbed. Finally I pulled away.

"Ugh, I got your shirt all wet," I joked.

"It's okay," he said, kissing my forehead.

"Shut up," I grinned and swatted him. Nick reached out for my face and cupped my chin.

"You're the best thing that's ever happened to me Monica," he whispered. There's something funny about saying goodbye. Sometimes you mean it, other times you don't. Some goodbyes mean good riddance, others see you later. But rarely goodbye is a preview of what is to come. You say goodbye and know, just know, it won't be the last time you'll ever see them. But like I've said before. Life's a pool. You never know when someone's going to splash and disrupt your perfect balance. But it's okay if someone splashes now. I'm ready for my imperfect balance.

"I know," I said playfully. Then Nick kissed me. I wanted to drink in that feeling. The feeling of happiness, comfort, warmth. A feeling I knew would go away when Nick wasn't with me. And a feeling I knew would return the minute I saw Nick again. Who knew, maybe we would even go to the same college next year.

"Last call for flight to Richmond, Virginia," A flight attendant announced.

"That's me," Nick sighed. I gave him a quick peck and watched him head after his parents. When he reached the gate, I saw him turn and wave at me. I waved back. He grinned then turned around. I watched the back of his head until he disappeared around the corner.

I set down the last box of my stuff in my room and wipe my brow. It's an extremely hot day in august which is not good for moving stuff from my old room at my dad's house to my new one at my grandma's.

"Monica? When you finish unpacking why don't you come downstairs for some cookies?" my grandma calls up to me.

"Okay," I yell down. I reach into the box and pull out my newly framed picture of my mom. I walk over to an empty space on the wall above my dresser and hang the picture there. I reach to the bottom of the box and hang up some more shirts in my closet. But when I turn, I notice the empty spot on my dresser. It's the space reserved for the first picture of Nick and me. A picture I have yet to take. But I realize now, that you can't just take a snapshot of life, framing it to preserve the memory. You have to carry the memory on, making it live again. That's what I have to do with my mom. If I just have a picture of her, she would be frozen, forever in that position, that time and place. I have to carry her in my heart. My heart will grow and change and allow new loves such as Nick, but in my heart my mother will live on. I take out the last things in the box and toss it into the pile of boxes besides the door.

"Monica, come down before your friends get here," my grandma yells up to me in her sweet voice.

"I'll be right down!" I shout back. I don't know why I didn't move in here right after my mother died. At least now I won't have to worry about my father. He's in rehab now but who cares? I sure don't. He's a character in my life that's finished in the story.

Kayce and Rachel are coming to sleepover later, but grandma is persistent that I eat the cookies before my friends do. It's her secret recipe. There are so many things I can't wait to tell my friends. But there are some things you just can't explain. They've never been in love, so how can I describe my feelings for Nick? I can't. But that's a good thing. People in a casual relationship can say, he makes me feel happy or loved. But one's with true love know there are not any words in a dictionary to describe what you feel. My heart not only soars when I see him, it flies. My stomach doesn't get butterflies, it gets hummingbirds. I don't get electricity, I get a storm.

My computer beeps, signifying that it has finally pulled up my search results on Maybreck Island. I have a dinosaur computer. I walk over to my desk and click on the first link. Almost instantly an article pops up about how Maybreck Island was in use for only two years before all the troops were sent home. I smile. So Fredrick and Mary *did* have a happy ending. Maybe I was right. Maybe the letter really did signify Nick and my relationship. If absence makes the heart grow fonder, then Nick and I will be okay. I turn to face my window, my hand automatically going towards my neck to clutch my diamond heart necklace. The minute my fingers clasp it, my cell phone rings. I reach over to my bed where I had dropped it. The caller id reads Nick.

The boat jolts against the dock with such force, a woman stumbles to find her husband's hand. He laughs as she clasps it.

"Nervous?" He asks. The woman glances at his pure blue eyes that she's been staring at for the last thirteen years.

"Not anymore," she grins and her husband pulls her close.

"Lucy?" she calls out to the little girl clutching the railing. The little girl turns, excitement pooling in her blue eyes. They looked exactly like her fathers. Lucy bounds over, her brown ponytail swaying with every step.

"We're here! We're here!" She cheers in her three year old voice. The woman her husband laugh and she swings her little girl up on to her hip, against her slightly protruding belly.

"Yeah, we're back," she turns to her husband as they step on to the familiar sand. So far the island looks the same except for a white sandy path that I leads to the pool.

"You ready?" her husband questions and squeezes her hand.

"Definitely," they walk down the path into the slightly bigger clearing. Memories came flooding back as she is happy to see that not much had changed. There are more huts and a life guard is at the pool but other than that, it looks exactly the same. There are strangers on vacation everywhere until the women spots a few familiar faces.

"Monica! Nick!" Caroline calls and waved from the old living room hut. The couple rushes over excitedly. They are the last ones to arrive. Calvin sits on one couch with the two year old twins Sarah and Calvin Jr. on his lap and Caroline's hand in his. Bidziil and Emilia sit on another couch both talking to Emilia's large stomach. Colby and Bethany are already going at it, sucking face in the corner. It is a good thing their wedding is soon.

Hugs are exchanged and although it was only a couple months since Nick and Monica last saw them, it felt like an eternity. Monica glances around at her friends and remembers those months they spent on this island. She remembers how they desperately wanted to leave. But coming back there for vacation felt like coming home.

Made in the USA
Lexington, KY
04 February 2012